SIREN CALL

A PROF CROFT PREQUEL 2

BRAD MAGNARELLA

Copyright © 2018 by Brad Magnarella

All rights reserved.

No part of this book may be reproduced in any form or by any electronic or mechanical means, including information storage and retrieval systems, without written permission from the author, except for the use of brief quotations in a book review.

Cover image by Damonza.com

bradmagnarella.com

THE PROF CROFT SERIES

PREQUELS
Book of Souls
Siren Call

MAIN SERIES
Demon Moon
Blood Deal
Purge City
Death Mage
Black Luck
Power Game
Druid Bond
Night Rune
Shadow Duel
Shadow Deep
Godly Wars
Angel Doom

SPIN OFFS
Croft & Tabby
Croft & Wesson

MORE COMING!

1

"Who is she?" Claire demanded.

I looked around in confusion. "Who's who?"

Her dark hair dropped across her left eye as she tilted her head impatiently. She was standing in the doorway to her bedroom. I was sitting on the edge of her bed, my shirt unbuttoned to my navel. We'd been rounding first on our way to second when her phone rang. She'd taken the call in the other room. When she returned, her body was as rigid as an iron poker.

"All right, let's back up," she said. "Where were you Saturday night?"

I could feel my anticipation of just a few minutes before leaving me like hot air from a balloon. So much for sliding into home. Not only that, I sensed a trap. Claire was an attorney.

"I thought we had this conversation," I said.

"Yes, and you told me you were tied up with work stuff."

"That's right," I said, giving her a look that asked, *And...?*

"All right, so why did Ellen just tell me she saw you leave

an apartment on West Ninety-second at eleven o'clock and get into a cab?" Her words were tight and clipped.

"Why did she think that was me?"

"Because you stopped and said hello!"

Damn, I had done that.

"I want to know who she is. And if you tell me a colleague, I'm going to pull the address for everyone on staff at Midtown College to see if any of them live on West Ninety-second."

"You'll do what?"

"So let me ask again. Who is she?"

Claire and I had met two months earlier at my favorite Midtown deli. With a short break between class and office hours, I'd run over to pick up a turkey club to go. Thinking I was looking for a table in the crowded deli, Claire invited me to sit at hers. I considered the invitation, and the startlingly fresh-faced woman in the business skirt doing the inviting, and accepted.

And now here we were, navigating the first shoals of doubt from which there was usually no recovery.

"There's no she," I said.

"Then why did you lie to me?"

"I didn't lie. But, all right, I wasn't completely honest, either. I have a second job. That's what I was doing on Ninety-second Street."

Claire surprised me with a sharp laugh. "A second job that you've managed to keep a secret from me all this time? What, pray tell, is this second job? Pizza deliverer? Male gigolo? Masked avenger?"

Her last guess wasn't too far off, actually—excepting the mask, of course. I thought about the nether creature I had banished in the Upper West Side apartment that Saturday night, how I'd blasted the bug into gobs of phlegm and then given the young man who had called it up a stern lecture on the dangers of conjuring. I'd incinerated his spell book in front of him to underline the point. Probably overkill given the man's terror, but I'd been in a weird mood.

"I help people," I said at last.

"Help people," Claire repeated, crossing her arms.

For a moment, I considered telling her the truth. But Chicory had warned me about revealing my true identity. Wizards made compelling targets, and if word got out, I'd not only be endangering myself but those closest to me. Also, I'd been with Claire long enough to know she didn't believe in the supernatural. She'd either think I was joking or off my rocker.

"Before I was a college professor, I underwent ... other training."

She circled a hand for me to continue.

I opened my mouth, then hesitated. I thought about my summer on Lazlo's farm in Romania five years earlier. With his help, I'd developed my mental prism, learned to hone and push energy through it, to cast my first invocations. Upon returning to New York, I was handed off to Chicory and tasked with banishing nether creatures like the bug I'd exploded on Saturday night. But how in the hell was I going to spin all of that to Claire?

"Look, does it really matter?" I snapped.

"Yes, because it's not just Saturday. You've made excuses in the past for disappearing that in hindsight..."

Claire's mouth was still moving, but I could no longer hear what she was saying. A foghorn was going off in my head. I winced and clamped my temples. My alarm, meaning the wards had picked up another breach. I pawed the side of the bed for my grandfather's cane and stood.

"I've gotta go," I said as the noise subsided.

"If you leave, don't bother calling me again."

I tapped toward her, faking a slight limp. "Look, I'm really sorry."

"I'm serious, Everson."

Claire shrank from my attempted kiss. Under different circumstances, I would have stayed and tried some damage control, but there wasn't time. A breach meant another creature was loose in the city and lives were in danger. I would call her when it was over. There was a lot about Claire I really liked, and I'd hate for this to end over a misunderstanding.

I was almost to the apartment door when something hit me in the center of the back. I wheeled and looked from the mess on the floor to Claire's flushed face. A wall of fragrance rose between us.

"Did you just throw your potpourri at me?"

"Get out," she said.

"Yeah, I was trying to."

I left the apartment before she could throw anything else and jogged to the elevator. It was over. The relationship had lasted a little longer than most since I'd started spell-slinging, and a little less than others. My record was four months, but that had been almost four years ago.

Lazlo had said wizarding would be a lonely road, and man, he hadn't been kidding.

As the elevator started down, a gray melancholy formed inside me like a stone, its weight seeming to speed my descent. I looked around the empty car. Was this what I had to look forward to for a life?

2

I paid the cabbie his fare plus an after-dark premium and stepped onto the garbage-blown sidewalk at Broadway and Forty-second. It was after midnight, and the night creatures were out and about: pimps, prostitutes, drug dealers, and the desperate, as well as the destitute, who had nowhere else to go.

"You sure this is where you wanna be dropped?" the cabbie asked.

I had used the empty mailroom in the lobby of Claire's apartment building to cast a hunting spell. The spell had aligned my cane to the location of the breach, and this was where it had pulled me. When I turned, I found the cabbie peering from his rolled-down window at what had become of Times Square.

"Unfortunately." I said.

He shook his head as though to say *good luck*, and took off.

I stood in the marquee lights of one of the adult movie theaters and looked around. It was hard to believe that only five years earlier this had been one of the most valuable blocks of real estate in the world. But the financial crash had hit New York like a wrecking ball, and Times Square was on the front line. As tourism dollars evaporated, businesses pulled up stakes. The big companies left first, sending rents plummeting. When organized crime and the vice trades moved in, the few storefronts that had managed to hang on either shut down or got taken over. The scene had come to resemble a 1970s version of Times Square, and that wasn't good.

"Hey, baby. Looking for a date?"

A young woman in a short leather skirt sauntered from the shadows. When she entered the marquee lights, her pale skin shone like porcelain. She held my gaze until she was standing in front of me, a hand bracing her cocked hip. For a moment, I forgot why I'd come down here.

"Like what you see?" she asked in a way that sounded like a dare.

The woman *was* striking, but her smile didn't come close to her glinting eyes. As she stepped nearer, a coldness radiated from her, suggesting vampire. When she reached up to caress my cheek, I went rigid. Her long nails whispered over my stubble.

"Oh, baby," she purred. "You're lonely. So, so lonely. You poor thing. But it doesn't have to be that way."

Her touch moved like smoke through the despair I had felt back at Claire's apartment. It promised intimacy, understanding—love, even. A kaleidoscope of erotic images pulsated through my thoughts and got my heart racing. When my eyelids started to flutter, I seized her icy hand and pulled it off me.

"No thanks," I said firmly.

"Are you sure, baby? You don't know what you're missing."

"Stay away from me."

I turned and followed the pull of my cane. When I'd gone

a short distance, I peeked back to make sure the creature wasn't following me. But she'd latched onto some lanky guy with glasses who had just come out of the theater.

Beyond them, I noticed a Cadillac parked curbside. Inside, a man in a lavender suit sat behind the wheel. His long, dark hair was parted in the center, and a pair of sunglasses hid his eyes. Her pimp. I didn't have to see his teeth to know his bulging lips hid fangs.

Like I said, the neighborhood had changed.

A block later, I found myself in front of a boutique hotel that advertised hourly as well as nightly rates. *Strange place for a conjuring*, I thought. The spell pulled me inside and toward a flight of stairs.

"Hey!" an unshaven guy at the small front desk called. "You got a room?"

"No," I admitted.

"Then you can't go up."

"How much for an hour?"

"Twenty bucks."

I pulled two tens from my wallet and swapped them for a room key. The guy gave me a look as though to say *By yourself?* Shrugging, he turned his ample body back to whatever he'd been watching on his portable TV. I pocketed the key without looking at the room number.

My cane pulled me up two grimy flights, then down a long corridor. At the far end, the cane pivoted me toward a closed door. I dispersed the weakening hunting spell, unlatched the cane's handle from the ironwood staff, and drew out a glinting steel sword.

"Protezione," I whispered.

Fresh energy moved through my casting prism and into the staff. An opal inset at the staff's end swelled with white light that grew into a shield around me—my first line of defense. Holding my sword out of sight beside my leg, I rapped the door with the staff. When no one answered, I rapped again, harder.

"Hello?"

Still no answer. No movement, even.

I tried the door handle, surprised when it turned. An invocation ready on my lips, I threw the door open.

An enormous man lay spread eagle on the bed, eyes open, tongue lolling from one corner of his mouth. I darted my gaze around the small room before closing and locking the door behind me. The man's nakedness spoke to why he'd come up here, but he was alone now.

"Sir?" I said, easing toward him.

I prodded the man in the side of the belly with my staff. The tissue was stiff enough that I was sure he was dead. I hunkered down until my eyes were level with his torso. To my surprise, the dense forest of hair over his chest rose and fell in a shallow rhythm. I looked around the room. My alarm had indicated a breach. Where was the casting circle? Where were the spell implements? And if the man had called up a nether creature, why were his organs still intact?

Slow down, Everson. Breathe.

I was still relatively green, not used to curveballs. The training I had been promised post-Romania had amounted to almost none. Chicory only checked in a couple of times a year, usually to gripe or issue a warning about something that I hadn't even known was off limits in the first place. He never stayed long and was next to impossible to reach once he'd left. To say it was frustrating was an understatement. I had learned to depend less on Chicory, and the Order in general, and more on the growing collection of books in my library.

I took a deep breath and opened my wizard's senses. The room with its beige walls and drab décor seemed to step back as light-filled patterns from the astral realm glowed into view. The man's soul flapped, unmoored, around a ragged void. It was like something had lowered its head into his essence and taken a bite. A deep blackness where the piece of his soul had been rotated slowly, its epicenter below the man's gut.

I noticed a second swirling pattern at the foot of the bed, this one made of blood-red energy. When I tried to pull it into my staff, the energy dispersed and joined the flow of the room.

Dammit.

The energy would have been useful, but my invocations were still clumsy. Most likely, the energy had marked the remnants of whatever had been here. And being able to identify the *what* in *whatever* was the first step in stopping it. I was dealing with a different breed of creature, that was for sure. One that fed, not on vital organs, but soul essence. That would suggest a class of demon, though certain vampires were known to feed on soul essence too. I wondered if that's what the alarm had picked up. There were definitely enough vamps in the neighborhood.

I looked around some more before shifting my senses back. As the pattern of astral lights faded out, I touched my staff to the man's belly and uttered ancient Words. I couldn't heal a soul, but under the right conditions, a soul could heal itself. I was placing the man in the equivalent of a coma. To have a chance, he would need a solid week of rest in a hospital, where he could be hydrated intravenously and generally tended to. After several moments, a halo of gauzy white light took hold around him and I pinched off the spell.

Now to figure out what attacked him...

I inspected the man's body for bite marks or injuries, starting at his head. By the time I reached his feet, I'd found none, but I did notice something beside them—several long strands of red hair. I pocketed two of the hairs before turning to the man's clothes draped over the back of a chair. In his pants pockets, I found a wallet and phone.

I left the phone alone—my wizard's aura would only smoke it—and opened his wallet. A driver's license and union card identified him as Al Molarski. I looked through a small stack of business and reward cards in a side sleeve until I reached the bottommost one.

"Bingo," I whispered.

The red card with white lettering held the contact info for an escort named Tabitha. Probably the woman who'd been with him tonight.

I jotted the information into a small notepad I carried in my coat pocket. As a courtesy to the police, I returned everything, save the two hairs, exactly how I'd found them. Not that there was going to be much of an investigation. Word had gone out years before that if you chose to do business in Times Square after dark, you were on your own, even post mortem.

"Done already, huh?" the man at the front desk asked when I returned the key.

I ignored the remark. "Do you know a redhead named Tabitha?"

"Tabby? Yeah, I know her," he said, an edge of suspicion in his voice. "Who's asking?"

"A possible client. Was she just here?"

"Maybe."

That meant yes. "Know where I can find her?"

I had her number, but she didn't need to know I was looking for her. I wanted to be able to observe her first, to get a sense of her connection to what I'd just observed in the room. As one of the last to have been with Mr. Molarski, she topped my list of suspects.

"She's working," he said. "Ask around."

"Does she work any corner in particular?"

He winced in a way that suggested my questions were starting to irritate him. "Hey, bud, I just check people in and out. There's a twenty-four-hour diner called Tony's a couple blocks up the street. Some of the girls hang out there."

"Thanks," I said. "Oh, and I heard some commotion up in 312. Sounded like someone having a heart attack. You might want to take a look."

The man consulted a clipboard on his desk. "Yeah, he's past his checkout."

Oh, he's checked out, all right, I thought. *The question is by whom.*

Or what.

3

I made my way warily up the street. Car horns blared across Times Square, while gunfire cracked several blocks away. On the next corner, a preacher with a shock of dirty white hair screamed about sin and salvation. I was approached a few times—for "dates," drugs, and spare change—but I kept moving, my gaze sweeping the grimy sidewalks and lurid lights.

I was on the lookout for a redhead. The closest I came, though, was an orange kitten I startled as I skirted a box holding a homeless man. The kitten's ochre green eyes flashed up at me before it chirped a small meow and scampered into an alleyway. The next business happened to be the diner the hotel clerk had mentioned: Tony's. Moments later I was stepping through the front doors.

The diner was surprisingly busy for one a.m. Most of the tables and booths were filled, while a pair of cooks in white aprons worked spatulas behind a counter, sweat glistening over their hard-bitten faces. A mist of cigarette smoke stirred around me as I made my way inside.

I scanned the patrons. A few looked back, but most were

in their own worlds. Among the predominately human crowd, I picked up some fae auras as well as a couple of cold vampiric currents.

No redheads, though.

At the end of the counter, I took a seat. A large man with an impressive afro came over and stared down at me.

"Just a coffee," I said.

He grunted and moved away.

Trying not to appear conspicuous, I peered over a shoulder. I'd heard stories of the fate of Times Square, but I'd never been in the thick of it, especially after dark. Now here I was, sitting among the vampires, dark fae, and street-trade workers. All of them offered the same thing: wish fulfillment for a price. Even following the Crash, it remained a lucrative trade.

When the man returned with my coffee, I lowered my voice.

"Hey, um, has a girl named Tabitha been in here tonight?"

The man's brow collapsed over his eyes in thick ridges. "This is a family restaurant," he said without a hint of irony. "I don't allow those kinds of transactions in here. You want a girl, go back out on the street."

"No, no, I'm not asking for that reason. I just want to talk to her."

"I don't remember ever seeing you 'round here before."

"First time," I confessed.

He leaned forward until his nose was inches from mine. "Piece of advice, first timer? Watch who you deal with down here, or there won't be a second time." His words sounded threatening, but as he moved away, I wondered if he had meant them as a warning.

"Don't mind Tony. He's in a bad mood tonight."

I turned to find a young woman sitting on the stool next

to mine. The seat had been vacant a moment before, and I hadn't heard her come up. It was almost as if she'd manifested from the smoke around us. But I could see right away that she was fully human.

"Johanna," she said in introduction, holding out a hand.

Though her outfit pegged her as a call girl, she had the soft face and intelligent eyes of someone in college. Beautiful brown-green eyes. Her chestnut hair fell in waves past her shoulders, several braided strands forming a thin crown around her head. Under different circumstances, it was the kind of look I might have fallen for.

"Everson," I said, shaking her offered hand.

"Something I can help you with, Everson?"

I was about to rebuff her, like I'd done the vampire outside, but Johanna wasn't asking in the seductive manner of someone looking for business. It had come out an honest question.

"Actually, I'm looking for a girl named Tabitha."

She smirked. "Don't like what's in front of you?"

"N-no, I'm not asking for that reason," I stammered.

When Johanna laughed, I noticed the whiteness of her teeth. "Relax, I'm just messing with you. How about this? Have breakfast with me, and I'll tell you whatever you want to know."

"Why breakfast?"

She shrugged. "Why not?"

"Are you saying you know Tabitha?"

"Maybe."

"All right. Breakfast. But that's it."

"Hey, that's all I asked for." She whistled. "Tony! Pair of specials and a coffee."

The large man grunted and said something to the cooks. Johanna pulled a pack of cigarettes from her purse, drew one out expertly with her lips, and lit it. She held the pack toward me.

"I don't smoke."

"Sorry, the John Constantine look threw me."

"Oh, the coat." I couldn't help but snort a laugh.

With a smile, Johanna leaned back and blew her smoke away from me. Though I was still on my guard, there was something about her that put me at ease. And not in the enchanting way of the supernatural. I felt like I was back in college, hanging out with a coed.

"I know it's none of my business," I said, peering around before looking back at her. "But how did you end up here? You ... I don't know. You don't seem like you belong."

I caught a tensing around her eyes. "I could say the same about you."

"Fair enough. But I don't work here."

"No, but you're looking for someone who does."

"Know where I can find her?"

She smiled. "Subtle, Everson."

"Hey, you never said it had to wait until *after* breakfast."

"True. But if I give you what you want now, what's going to keep you from ditching me?" I hesitated long enough for her to aim her cigarette at me. "See? I know what I'm doing."

"All right, but what's the point of keeping me here in the first place?"

"How about conversation?"

"The diner's not exactly empty."

"I know them already." Johanna waved a hand. "I want novelty."

I cocked an eyebrow. "Novelty."

"Why don't you start by telling me what you do?"

"It's not very interesting."

"Try me."

I squinted at her to make sure she wasn't putting me on. But something in the angle of her head told me she genuinely wanted to know. "I teach ancient mythology and lore at the college level."

"You need a doctorate to teach, right? What was your dissertation on?"

"How do you know about doctorates and dissertations," I asked suspiciously.

She gave a teasing smile. "You first."

"Fine." I told her about my studies at Midtown College and my trip to Romania, where I'd found the lost manuscripts of Dolhasca. I took her through the journey to the monastery with my three traveling companions and how that had turned out, all three dead. Somewhere in there Tony brought our specials, some sort of egg, sausage, cheese, and hash brown mash-up that was surprisingly good.

By the time I finished talking, both of our plates were clean, and Johanna was staring at me as if I'd just sung a flawless operetta. My wizard's voice had worked on her some, but I had fallen into the story too. Maybe it was having someone listen so raptly. Claire had never expressed more than a polite interest in my field.

"That's one of the most amazing stories I've ever heard," she said. "I mean, the wolves alone…"

I laughed. "Yeah, it was a little touch and go there." I'd left out the details about the demons and magic, but I found a part of me wishing I could share those with her too. Something told me Johanna would have accepted them as readily as she'd done the rest of my story.

"So you're looking for Tabitha," she said abruptly. "Is she in trouble?"

"I don't know," I said, testing her to see if she knew something. "Is she?"

"Everyone's in some kind of trouble, but we look out for each other around her. It's part of the code." She nodded past me. "See Green Eyes over there? She's been watching to make sure you don't try anything funny."

I turned to find a tall woman with long white hair staring at me from a table. Her eyes were the luminous green of the fae. A petite African-American girl, who didn't look older than seventeen, sat beside her in a fur coat. The third chair was empty, probably the one Johanna had been sitting in.

"I have sensitive hearing," Johanna said. "I heard you asking about Tabitha."

"So this was, what, some kind of test?"

She smiled and took a drag on her cigarette.

"Did I pass?" I asked.

"I'm not sure yet. What do you want with her?"

I chose my words carefully. "I think she might be involved in something she can't control." Whether Tabitha was a creature whose appetite had grown beyond her or a mortal conjurer, I wasn't sure yet. But I had definitely sensed something supernatural around the unconscious man.

Johanna took another drag and squinted through the smoke as if she were assessing me. Having come to some decision, she said, "She's done working for the night, so you're not going to find her out there. If you come back tomorrow, though, there's a good chance you'll see her."

"Do you know where she lives?" I asked. "I'd like to talk to her tonight."

"We don't give out each other's addresses. That falls under the code too."

I nodded in understanding, but I was thinking about the hair in my pocket. I could use it to cast a hunting spell that would deliver me to Tabitha's door. Then I'd still have my element of surprise.

Johanna snapped her fingers in front of my face. "Hey, I know that look, and I'd put it out of your head. Some take the code seriously, and some take it *really* seriously. First timers who don't learn that usually don't come back a second time. Tony's not wrong there. And maybe it's selfishness, but I'd like to see you again."

"Me?" If Johanna had an angle, I hadn't figured it out yet. "Well, I can't promise I'll be a regular."

"But you'll be here tomorrow night?"

"It doesn't sound like I have a choice. What time would you suggest?"

"Tabitha usually goes out when it's dark, so after nine. I'll tell her I checked you out, but I can't guarantee she'll talk."

Since there was no chance now of observing Tabitha discreetly, I decided to go a little bolder. "Can you tell me anything about her? Where she's from, what she's like?"

Johanna took a thoughtful drag and peered toward the menu board but without reading it. "Hard to say. We all wear masks of one kind or another—it comes with the work—but I'm not sure anyone has really seen past hers. I know she's from the Midwest. Been here about as long as I have."

"Any idea what she was doing before?"

"You'll have to ask her."

"Guess I will," I said, pulling out my wallet.

Johanna moved her purse around to her lap. "It's on me, first-timer."

"I can't let you pay."

"Would you have gotten breakfast if I hadn't asked?"

"Well, no, but—"

"You can buy next time."

When I hesitated, she took my wallet from my hand, returned it to my back pocket, and gave it a pat. Once more, I wasn't picking up an act. It was more like we were old friends play-fighting over a bill.

I relented with a chuckle. "Fine."

When she smiled back, it touched something inside me. I thought about her out there with the vampires and the fae, not to mention the scummy human element, which could be even more dangerous.

"Hey," I said quietly. "Is there anything I can do for you?"

Maybe that had been her play the whole time, but I didn't care. I wanted to help her.

"Oh, don't start." She stubbed out her cigarette in an ashtray. "I have a social worker for that. I also have this." She drew out her necklace until a complex knot appeared from her shirt. "A charm against aggression." When I touched it, powerful protective energy pulsed from the silvery material.

"Where did you get it?" I asked.

"A gift from Green Eyes. Her name's Jade."

I had assumed the fae woman was another street walker, but was she Johanna's madam? It didn't seem appropriate to ask. I was just glad Johanna had people, and enchantments, looking out for her.

No doubt what had kept her alive.

I lowered my hand from the knot. "I meant what I said about helping."

Johanna's intelligent eyes softened as they peered into mine. "I know you did, Everson."

She shouldered her purse and returned to the table with Jade and the girl in the fur. It wasn't until I was in a cab heading back to the West Village that I realized Johanna had told me nothing about herself.

4

Back at my apartment, I stepped past my wards and triple-bolted the door behind me. Moonlight glowed through the two-story windows, giving my industrial loft unit a gray, cavernous look.

I felt empty suddenly. It wasn't just my relationship with Claire ending earlier that night. It was my encounter with Johanna. There had been a rare, almost electrical energy between us. An intimate sense of knowing the other, despite never having met, despite living in entirely different worlds.

And that's where the emptiness came from: knowing it could never be.

Sighing, I turned up the floodlights. I was physically tired and emotionally spent, but I wanted to learn *something* about this Tabitha before I called it a night. My footsteps echoed over the concrete floor as I crossed the unit to the ladder that climbed to my library/lab. I pulled myself up until I was facing a wall that held a growing collection of magical tomes and grimoires.

My focus tonight, though, was on the lab portion of the loft space.

I turned to a long table that ran along the loft's railing and sprinkled a circle of copper filings onto its iron surface. From my pocket, I removed one of the red hairs I had recovered from Al Molarski's grip and placed it at the circle's center. Aiming my cane, I incanted until the circle glowed with protective power. I did the same to a second circle inset in the floor, the one I would be casting from. Finally, I poised my cane over the hair and spoke the Word for reveal.

"Rivelare."

My cane stiffened. A moment later, the spell writhed from my cane's opal stone in threads of white light. The threads encircled the hair, exploring it, searching for essence to tease out. At my stage of wizarding, reveal spells were unpredictable. I might pick up traces of magic or hear the whisper of a name—I might even perceive a face. But after several moments, this spell gave me nothing. I watched the threads of light return to the opal.

C'mon, man.

I repeated the Word, pushing more power into it, but the hair only smoked and then popped into a flame.

"Shit," I muttered, dispelling the circle. Energy whooshed out, along with the foul smell of the burnt hair. Either I was too tired to effectively cast, or Tabitha had covered her tracks —which would suggest she wasn't an amateur at all. I considered running the reveal spell again, using the other hair in my pocket, but decided to save it in case I needed it for a hunting spell tomorrow night.

With nothing more to do, I took a shower and crawled into bed. I thought I would crash immediately, but the huge silence of the apartment kept me awake. That and visions of Johanna.

I slept until noon the next day, Saturday, and then spent the afternoon grading student papers. I watched the time. Johanna had suggested nine o'clock, but when I ran out of things to distract myself with around seven, I started getting ready. I had just finished loading up my trench coat when the alarm sounded.

Crap.

I rushed up to my library/lab and examined my magical hologram of the city. The hologram was pulsing red near where Broadway crossed Forty-second Street. I zoomed in to get a precise location. I didn't want to expend energy on a hunting spell if I didn't have to. The breach had occurred in the lower level of a parking garage north of the Port Authority Bus Terminal.

I sketched the location in my notepad, refilled my tube of copper filings, and grabbed my cane.

The graying man working the ticket booth at the garage looked like death warmed over. Fitting, considering the garage looked like a giant crypt. The man watched dully as I paid the cabbie and then jogged past him and down the graffiti-tagged ramp to the lower level.

When I was out of his view, I cast a shield and pulled my cane into sword and staff. Light glimmered from my protective enclosure, illuminating the cooling darkness. I breathed through pursed lips to counteract the phobia that was drawing my chest tight. It was the whole underground thing. Thick cement columns rose at intervals, giving the lot the appearance of catacombs.

In the southwest corner sat a lone vehicle, a brown van.

I crept toward it. The windows had fogged over, but I

could see the silhouette of a figure in the back. I knocked on the window, then opened the sliding door. A lanky man fell out onto the pavement. I jumped back, heart hammering. When I recovered my breath, I poked my head into the van to ensure it was empty before returning my attention to the victim.

He was stiff but breathing, just like the large man I'd found last night. A shift to my wizard's senses revealed the same soul damage and swirling blackness, the epicenter below his navel.

Given the van's location, and the unfastened state of the man's pants, it wasn't hard to piece together what had happened. He had picked up a girl and instead of paying for a twenty-dollar room had paid five to park down here. He had gotten his entertainment, and now he was soul drained, half dead.

I placed him in a restorative coma and then rolled him enough to draw his wallet from his back pocket. The driver's license ID'd him as James Virga. I noted the sheaf of bills that totaled almost one hundred dollars.

So, definitely not attacked for his money.

I replaced the wallet and searched the rest of him. Finding nothing notable, I left him to inspect his van. On the passenger's seat, between the headrest and body, I spotted a snagged length of red hair. I pulled out the one I'd recovered from the hotel room the night before and held them side by side. Perfect match, meaning Tabitha had been here as well.

I drew the snagged hair free, pocketed it, and stood back to take in the entire scene.

Two stiffs—pun absolutely intended—and so far Tabitha's the common denominator.

I returned the man to how I'd found him, once more to give the police their fair crack. But I saw an urgency where the NYPD wouldn't. Namely that something had breached our world and dined on another soul, meaning the being was becoming more powerful at the same time it was weakening the barrier that protected our plane from all sorts of subaltern nasties.

But if this Tabitha had called the being up, how was she doing it? And why?

I crossed the lot at a fast walk, intent on having the old man in the booth call an ambulance for the victim. I also wanted to know what he'd witnessed.

I was halfway to the ramp when a tall, slender figure stepped from behind a cement pillar. He walked with a cane, not unlike mine. In a flash, he was standing in the light of my shield, a grin touching his lips.

"What's your hurry?" he hissed.

I noted the center-parted hair that fell to the shoulders of his green suit. It was the same man I'd seen in the parked car the night before—the pimp. Only this time, I didn't have to guess at his true nature.

His fangs flashed as he flew toward me.

5

Though my shield protected me, the vampire's violent collision knocked me from my feet. I sailed several parking spaces before hitting the ground and then tumbling into the back wall of the lot. Before I could get up, the vampire was on top of me. Sparks fell over my face as he gashed at my shield.

"Respingere!" I cried.

Power gathered in my shield and then detonated with a bright pulse. The vampire threw a forearm to his eyes as the force blasted him off me. He crunched into the back corner of a parked station wagon, sending it skidding. Glass from the shattered rear window spilled over him.

I gained my feet as he pushed himself to his. Adrenaline pumped through me. The vampire glared back at me, hanks of hair hanging over his red eyes.

"I-I thought wizards and vampires had a truce," I stammered.

I'd only encountered a handful of vampires during my time in New York, partly because they weren't my beat, and partly because of the referenced truce. Centuries before, vampires and my magic-wielding forebears had aligned against the enforcers of the Inquisition. My grandfather had stored the power of the so-named *Brasov Pact* in a ring that would punish violators of the truce. A ring I presently wore. But as I glanced down at the embossed image of a rearing dragon, I noticed the ring hadn't come to life. Which meant this vampire belonged to a different strain than the one my grandfather had fought alongside.

As if to underscore this, the vampire hissed, "You were mistaken," and flew at me again.

This time, I was ready. *"Vigore!"* I shouted.

The force that shot from my sword stopped him cold. With a clenched jaw, I twisted the force so that it lifted the vampire straight into the air and then pile-drove him head first against the floor. He grunted as the garage shuddered around us. With another Word, I encased him in a shield like mine. The vampire recovered quickly and thrashed against his confinement.

I pushed energy into it as I strode toward him.

"Who are you?" I demanded, hiding the effort I was having to exert. I could feel Thelonious's creamy presence around my thoughts, could feel the incubus waiting for me to weaken enough so he could rush in and use my body as a vessel. "Why are you attacking me?"

The vampire struggled some more, a ring with a thick purple gem pulsing away on his finger. I sensed magic coming off the ring, but it was ineffective against my own. The vampire stopped suddenly.

"Who are *you*?" he shot back. "And why are you preying on our clients?"

"Preying on your clients?"

"Last night, I watched you walk into the Lincoln Hotel and then leave ten minutes later. The same hotel where a man was later found in a coma. And tonight, here you are, leaving the scene of another attack." His eyes cut to the parked van. "I can smell the magic on the unconscious man from here."

"Hold on a sec. I'm *investigating* the attacks."

He continued as if I hadn't spoken. "Despite appearances to the contrary, Times Square is relatively safe after dark. Do you know why? Because we have a *vested* interest in that safety. The reason should be self-evident, but there's a saying amongst us: 'Scared clients stay away, and dead clients don't pay.'"

"Oh, so your little vampiress who approached me last night had no intention of sucking me dry?"

"She might have snuck a taste. Your blood *is* potent, wizard. Intoxicatingly so." His narrow nostrils flared as a pale tongue licked his lips. He then grinned enough to show his fangs. "But repeat business is worth more to us than a temporary sating of the appetite. *That's* where the profits are."

"Is that so?" I asked thinly.

"And if word gets out that clients are paying with their lives, guess where the business goes?" He made a fluttering motion with his fingers. "Far, far away."

"Well, you're barking up the wrong—"

The vampire lunged so suddenly he almost caught me off guard. I incanted to reinforce his wobbling shield and bore down.

"I'm not doing what you think I'm doing, *goddammit*," I said through gritted teeth. "Last night I was alerted to a breach that led me to the hotel, all right? Same thing happened today, pulling me here. Someone or something is devouring these people's souls. And the only thing that seems to connect them is someone named Tabitha. Do you know her?"

The vampire had continued to struggle as I spoke, but when I said the name, he stopped.

"Tabitha," he repeated.

"Yeah, she apparently works the streets. Has red hair."

"I've never trusted her."

"Why not?"

He was about to answer before appearing to remember his confinement. His eyes glared anew.

"I'll release you if you promise not to attack me," I said. My defensive magic was strong enough to keep him at bay, but I didn't want to have to expend power unnecessarily. "I'm *not* the person offing these guys."

The vampire gave a slight nod.

With a Word, I dispersed his confinement. The vampire gained his feet with preternatural speed but then took his time removing a pair of gold-framed sunglasses from his breast pocket and donning them. Remaining a safe distance back, I tamped my own shield down, but kept it in place.

Noting my caution, the vampire grinned.

"I believe you, and do you want to know why?" he asked. "You're no killer."

I was pretty sure the vampire hadn't meant it as a compliment, but I thanked him anyway, mostly out of relief. "I'm Everson."

"Drake," he answered.

"Good to meet you, Drake," I said as a formality. "Now, about Tabitha. Why don't you trust her?"

"'Cause she's a free agent."

"What does that mean exactly?"

"It means she doesn't have representation."

"No pimp?"

"You're a quick study. And she's had offers—generous ones. My own included."

"Is she a vampire?"

"A mortal."

"Doesn't working for herself mean she keeps all of what she makes? What am I missing? I mean, why pay you a share if she doesn't have to?"

Drake grinned. "You're missing a lot, Everson. I spoke about our interest in our clients' safety. Same goes for our girls. No girls, no clients. No clients, no money. You follow?"

"Yeah?"

"You saw me last night. Probably didn't look to you like I was doing much, but I had my senses trained on five girls—the one you so indecorously turned away, and four others, two of them mortal. The instant I hear trouble, I'm there. Could be a client getting too rough, could be a vamp thinking he's found some low-hanging fruit, could be any number of things."

"So you keep them safe."

"Not only that, I handle any difficulties, legal or other."

"And Tabitha rejected that help."

"Multiple times. Girls try the solo routine from time to time. Most give up after their first bad experience, or they disappear. That usually happens in the first month. But Tabitha's been out here for years."

I remembered what Johanna told me last night about the code. "Well, maybe she has other people looking out for her."

"The other girls?" He snorted. "Not while they're working."

I saw his point. They couldn't keep tabs on each other all night. If Tabitha was on her own, odds were she had supernatural assistance.

"Have you ever seen her with anyone?" I asked.

"Oh, all the girls around here mingle with one another. I don't care for it myself. I don't want my girls getting any ideas.

But what can I do? I have to keep them happy." He spoke with an aggrieved air, but his stance toward the girls as property disgusted me. *He* disgusted me.

"But have I seen Tabitha with anyone other than them?" he asked with a grin. He could sense my discomfort. "I can't say that I have, Everson. Not that I've paid her much attention."

"Well, look, I'm going to try to find and talk to her tonight. See what the connection is to the two men. We don't know anything yet, so let's keep our cool, all right?"

"I don't have your patience for due process, Everson. I can't afford to. Scared clients stay away, and dead clients don't pay, remember? That Tabitha was with both men is enough for me. She's putting the livelihood of myself, my girls, and everyone who works down here in jeopardy."

I checked my watch. Johanna had said Tabitha wouldn't be out till nine, but it looked like she'd started early if the evidence in the van was anything to go by.

"Give me until midnight," I said.

"Ten," the vampire countered.

"Eleven."

"Ten," he repeated.

I couldn't see past his sunglasses, but I could imagine his predatory eyes, the pinpoint pupils. Ten was the best I was going to get. It was almost eight now, which meant I had a little over two hours.

"Fine," I said, and hurried up the ramp.

6

The old man at the ticket booth confirmed a "young gal" with red hair had left the garage about thirty minutes before I'd arrived. Now it was a matter of finding her. As an ambulance siren started in the distance, I peered east toward Times Square. Traffic was picking up. Maybe I'd catch her working one of the corners.

I joined up with Broadway and walked three blocks north of Forty-second Street, then several blocks south. It was a similar scene to last night's. But though plenty of girls were out soliciting, none had red hair. Neither would they give me any info on Tabitha's whereabouts. They either ignored me, not wanting to send business to a competitor, or turned coy, which I didn't have time for.

I kept an eye out for Johanna too. I told myself it was because she could help me, but who was I kidding? The pull I felt toward her was as irresistible as it had been last night. And irrational. Anyway, I didn't see her. I did catch Drake's brown Cadillac rolling past. As if to remind me of my deadline, he grinned and shot me a finger pistol before pulling away.

At nine o'clock, I decided it was time to cast a hunting spell. The only reason I'd put it off was in the hopes I'd conserve power by spotting Tabitha first. My encounter with Drake had cost me.

I ducked into the alley behind Tony's diner, stepping over a pair of junkies. At the alley's end I found a spot hidden from street view by a Dumpster. Pulling my vial of copper filings from a pocket, I sprinkled out a casting circle and pushed some power into it. I then set the other hair I'd retrieved last night into the circle's center.

I peeked around the Dumpster to make sure no one was coming and held my cane over the hair.

"*Seguire,*" I whispered.

The cane trembled in my grasp as power coursed through it and reached for the hair's essence. The spell would pull the essence into the cane, and the hunt would be on. But instead of essence, I got smoke. The hair popped into a flame, just like last night.

"Not again, *dammit,*" I whispered.

By the time I stamped out the flame, the hair had shriveled into a brittle crisp. I dropped the final hair, the one I'd recovered from the car, into the circle and tried again. The result was the same: smoke and flame, but no spell. I was out of hairs, and I had nothing else that belonged to her.

As I swept the circle apart, something moved to my right. I spun, heart hammering. But it was just the orange kitten I'd seen last night, scampering around a stack of wooden pallets. With a sigh, I pulled out my pocket notepad and flipped to the page where I'd written down Tabitha's number. I'd make a quick stop into Tony's and then give her a call.

The diner wasn't nearly as crowded as it had been the night before—I guessed most of the regulars were just starting their shifts. I scanned the patrons for any redheads.

None in here either, but I did spot Johanna's two friends from last night, Jade and the young woman in the fur coat, at a table near the back. Jade's green eyes stared at me as I approached.

"Hey, uh, do you mind if I join you for a minute?" I asked.

"Sure," Fur Coat said meekly, then peeked over at Jade, as if seeking approval.

Jade remained staring at me for another moment before giving the barest nod. She brought a cigarette in a sleek cigarette holder to her mouth, then tossed her long white hair to one side as she exhaled through pursed lips. The fragrance of the smoke was too sweet to be tobacco. When a subtle wave of bliss washed over me, I recognized it as wicki weed from the faerie realm.

"Jade, right?" I said, leaning away from the smoke. When she didn't answer, I turned to Fur Coat. "I'm sorry, but I didn't get your name last night."

"It's Candy," she replied, dipping her chin and issuing a sheepish smile. She spoke with a southern accent. My heart started to break for the child—a runaway most likely—but then I sensed a glamour around her. She was older than she appeared, possibly much older.

"Good to meet you. I'm Everson." Candy accepted my handshake, her grip small and lacking confidence.

"What do you want?" Jade asked abruptly.

Candy pulled her hand from mine as though she'd been chastised.

"I'm actually looking for Tabitha," I said.

"Don't you mean Johanna?" Jade asked knowingly.

"Well, yeah. Her too."

While the wicki smoke seemed not to effect Jade or Candy, I became aware that it was making me grin. The diner suddenly seemed incredibly lovely. I wanted to hug everyone: the women at my table, the patrons around us—hell, even the cooks. The urgency to find Tabitha suddenly felt very distant. As an enchanted weed, wicki had that effect.

"Do you know where I can find her? I mean, them?" I stammered.

Candy giggled, but Jade's expression remained flat as her eyes fixed on mine through the haze. "What's your interest in Johanna?"

"I met her last night at the counter." I gestured vaguely behind me. "You saw us. I just wanted to..."

What *did* I want?

"She's working," Jade replied coldly.

"For you?" I asked a little too pointedly.

Jade rolled her eyes and looked away, as if she wanted nothing more to do with me. Probably just as well. I was wasting my time here. I needed to find a payphone and call Tabitha.

"Well, thanks for your help," I said, standing. "Good to meet you, Candy."

She responded with another of her shy smiles. "You too, Everson," she practically whispered.

My head didn't clear until I'd stepped back outside. I checked my watch. Ten after nine. I hurried a block north to where I remembered seeing a payphone. My nose wrinkled as I drew back the folding door and stepped into the booth, which apparently doubled as a community restroom.

I pulled my notepad from my coat, dropped two quarters into the slot, and dialed Tabitha's number. The smoky voice that answered was much like I'd imagined it would sound, but it wasn't live.

"*Hey, baby,*" the recording said. "*I'm so sorry I missed your call, but if you leave your name, number, and what you're looking for, I'll get back to you just as fast as I can.*" A simple message, but full of suggestion. She was good.

When the tone sounded, I cleared my throat. I considered giving my real name, but if Tabitha had decided she didn't want to talk to me, I'd be out of luck.

"Yeah, this is Jack," I said, affecting a deep voice for no good reason. I leaned toward the phone box to read the number, but someone had scratched it out. "I, ah, don't have a phone on me, but I'm in Times Square and I really want to meet you. I'll be waiting on the corner of Broadway and Forty-third. If you're there by nine-thirty, I'll pay double your normal price. Thanks."

I hung up, hoping the promise of a bonus would work. It was all I had.

I opened the door and jumped, startled to find Candy standing right outside the booth.

"Jesus," I said, pressing a hand to my chest. "You scared the hell out of me."

"I know where she is," she said in a lowered voice.

"Who, Tabitha?"

Candy took my hand, waited for a break in the traffic, and then pulled me after her. She apparently didn't buy my gimpy act, which I used as an excuse to carry my cane. We crossed the street at a run, cutting between honking cars and cabs. From there we jogged up to Forty-fourth Street and then toward Eighth Avenue. Candy was surprisingly fast, given her short legs and high heels.

"Where are we going?" I asked.

"She wanted me to bring you to her without Jade knowing."

A break, finally, I thought. But as the street darkened and the foot traffic thinned, I remembered Tony's warning about watching who I dealt with down here. Had Jade sent her underling to silence me or something? Candy stopped suddenly at an unassuming metal door and knocked. I whispered a shield invocation, remaining tense until I felt the air harden around me.

A moment later, a door slid back from a slot at eye level. From inside, music thumped and blue and pink lights flashed through a wall of smoke. A deep set of eyes peered out at me before cutting to Candy.

"He's cool," Candy said, sounding a little too street smart.

The eyes moved back to mine. "Twenty-five," a deep voice said.

"Twenty-five?" I repeated.

"Dollars," Candy explained. "It's the cover to get in."

"This is a club?"

Candy nodded slowly, eyebrows raised like she was dealing with a naïve ten-year-old, but I still didn't entirely trust the situation.

"Twenty-five is kind of steep," I hedged.

"It's to keep out the riffraff," she said. "Do you want to see her or not?"

I pulled a twenty and five from my wallet and held them up. A blue-tinted hand with thick fingers plucked them from my grasp and retreated back into the slot. The door slid closed and bolts clanged. Just when I thought I'd been fleeced, the entire door opened and an ogre waved for me to enter.

Crap. A fae club.

I looked back to see if Candy was coming too, but she was already heading back to Times Square.

"You coming in or not?" the ogre asked.

The mist and lights around him had a similar enchanting effect as the wicki weed Jade had been smoking. I resisted their pull. But if Tabitha was inside...

The ogre grunted and started to swing the door closed.

"Wait!" I cried. Before I could second-guess myself, I darted through the opening. The door clanged behind me, narrowly missing my coattail. The ogre waved a wooden paddle around me. When it passed over my coin pendant and cane, runes in the paddle glowed. The ogre didn't appear concerned. With a final grunt, he lowered the paddle, secured the giant bolts in the door, and settled back onto his stool.

The club was a large room of bouncing bodies. At the far end, above the main mass of dancers, a DJ dressed in white athletic gear worked two turntables with four arms. *Has to be a glamour*, I told myself. But anything seemed possible in here. The throbbing sound, coupled with the lights and mist, had insinuated themselves into my neurochemistry to produce a blissfully hypnotic effect.

I felt my shield dissolve as I drifted toward the dancers. Soon I was in the center of the dance floor, bouncing among them. The crowd was mostly made up of humans, but I spotted several fae. All that mattered, though, was that we were having a great time. Maybe the greatest of our lives. I suddenly loved all creatures—light, dark, whatever. There were probably vamps in here as well, and you know what? I didn't care. I loved them too.

Every time I bounced against another body, pleasure hormones exploded through me. When I laughed, it was with the recklessness of a child, nothing like my normal laughter. And it felt awesome.

"Here," someone said into my ear. "Drink this."

I accepted the bottle without question and drank the rest of it down. Whatever it was tasted fizzy and wonderful and seemed to quench every cell in my body. I turned to thank whoever had given it to me—and kiss them while I was at it. Even if it was an ogre, it wouldn't matter, I decided. But when

I turned, I found myself looking at the most beautiful being I'd ever seen.

"Miss me?" Johanna asked, her mouth tilting into a smile.

The hair that fell over her shoulders in rivulets was secured at the top with a blue wrap, giving her a gypsy-like appearance. Her peasant blouse and jeans completed the look. I stared, too overcome to say anything. She stepped into my arms, and we rocked to the beat, our hips and legs bumping against each other. I leaned my face back and let the flashing lights bombard my pupils. Every pulse felt like a direct injection of bliss. I was pretty far from happy-go-lucky in my normal life, but now I couldn't stop smiling.

"That was Nehi Grape," Johanna said into my ear. "It counteracts the fae magic in here for some reason. Give it a minute and you'll feel more like yourself."

"No," I said, burying my face into her sweet-smelling neck. "I don't ever want this to end."

She laughed. "You don't want to lose your mind either."

As the seconds passed, the lights and sounds settled into a more normal club experience until I was no longer so blissed-out, no longer so in love with the people around me. When I felt a vampire's chilly aura, I edged away. Johanna still looked and felt amazing, but I thought about what she'd just told me. Jesus, I *had* been losing my mind, hadn't I?

I bit back my Jokeresque smile and used my coat sleeve to wipe Nehi from the sides of my mouth. "Thanks."

"So Candy found you, huh?"

"Candy? Yeah, how did you know?"

"I told her to bring you here."

"Wait, that was you?" I checked my watch and looked wildly around. "I thought I was coming to meet Tabitha."

Johanna grasped the sides of my head until I was looking

into those strikingly intelligent eyes. "Relax, she's coming. I set up a meeting."

"Will she be here by ten?" I asked.

Nodding, she took my hand and led me from the dance floor to a corridor I hadn't seen upon entering. Another ogre undid a velvet stanchion, and we passed through what must have been an enchantment, because I could no longer hear the noise of the club. It was replaced by the sedate voices and clinking glasses of a VIP lounge. Well-dressed men and women sat at a circular bar being tended by a striking faerie who could have been a man or a woman. The patrons' tall glasses held drinks of various enchanting colors.

"This way," Johanna said, leading me through a doorway off the corridor.

We entered a private room with a leather love seat and a small table with two tall drinks already poured. We sank into the couch, and Johanna nestled against me. I put my arm around her. We were facing the wall opposite the door, which had been glamoured to make it appear as if we were gazing out over Paris at night. Faint French chatter and cabaret music rose from what sounded like a café at street level. In the distance, the Eiffel Tower glimmered majestically.

"Wow," I said. "How did you swing this?"

"I called in some favors."

"Do I want to know?"

"Probably not."

"So ... you're not working tonight?"

"I cut out early."

"And that's cool with Jade?"

She looked up at me. "What does Jade have to do with anything?"

"I just thought she was your, you know..."

"My pimp?"

"Well, technically she'd be your madam."

Johanna laughed and ran a hand down the front of my face. "She's a friend. An overprotective friend, granted, but she doesn't manage me."

"Oh," I said, feeling stupid. I changed the subject. "And you're sure Tabitha's coming?"

"Definitely, but I was hoping we could steal a few minutes to ourselves." She kissed my neck until she reached my ear, giving it a playful bite, then settled her head back against my shoulder. I stroked her hair.

"That feels nice," she said, closing her eyes.

"So, I have to ask," I said after a moment. "Why this life?"

"Because I'm stubborn," she murmured.

"Is that all I'm going to get? You told me nothing last night."

Johanna remained quiet for a moment. In the glamour, silvery clouds slid over the moon while laughter rose from the French café. "I came to New York to escape," she said at last.

7

"Escape what?" I asked.

"This is going to sound stupid," she said with a sigh. "I used to dance ballet. My mother trained me, and my father was my manager. They'd both grown up in the ballet world. That's how they met. They started young with me. It was all ballet, all the time. My earliest memories were of doing straddle splits in our home studio. I competed, I won. But it was never enough for them. By the time I was a senior in high school, I felt like I was in a prison of their making. I had to get the hell out of there. They wanted me to go to this prestigious dance academy, but I applied to NYU in secret. I wanted to study visual anthropology. And damned if I didn't get in. I think Admissions liked my ballet background." She snorted dryly.

"When I finally summoned the courage that summer to tell my parents, they freaked out. Predictably. I'd get no support from them, they told me. In fact, if I was going to be so thankless, I could leave right then. So I did. I can still remember sitting in my packed car, preparing to back out of the driveway. I came so close to chickening out, Everson.

That's when my father said, 'Let's see how long you last.' There was this malice in his voice I'll never forget. I backed down the driveway and drove through the night until I got here."

"What happened with school?"

"At first, everything fell into place. The school let me get a dorm room early and enroll in summer term. When I explained my situation, they set me up with a work-study program that would pay most of my tuition. Between that and a waitressing job, I'd have enough. It was like I was meant to be there."

"And then the Crash happened," I said.

"Yep, and there went both sources of income."

"I'm really sorry."

"I thought about going home, but I kept hearing my father's voice. 'Let's see how long you last.' I couldn't let him win. So I sold my car, dropped out of school, and looked for a place to stay. I told myself it would be temporary. When the economy recovered, I'd just re-enroll. All I knew was that I couldn't go home. I wasn't even willing to leave the city. I didn't want to cede anything to my parents. They'd controlled me long enough."

My fingers left her hair and began stroking her arm.

"I ended up in an apartment with Jade and another girl. It was pretty obvious what they did, but the rent was cheap, and they didn't bring their work home. I'd made enough from the car sale that I could afford three months' rent, plus living expenses. But when three months came and went, and I still hadn't found any work, I talked to Jade. Strictly exotic dancing. No contact, though the clients could contact themselves all they wanted." She made a face. "Once again, I told myself it would be temporary. But one month became one year, then two, then three..."

Her voice trailed off.

"You should call your parents," I said.

"I know. But I can't."

"Have you tried?"

"I've thought about it. But then I hear what my father said. I see his face. I see my mother standing beside him, both of them wanting me to fail. I just ... I can't bring myself to do it. I haven't talked to them since I left."

My fingers had been working their way up under the edge of her sleeve as she spoke, but now they stopped. "What's this?" I asked, pulling the sleeve up over a fresh ridge of scar tissue.

Johanna straightened the sleeve and sat up suddenly. "It's nothing," she answered, her voice taking on an odd slant. She looked from me to the door. "I'm going to run to the restroom."

I checked my watch, surprised to find it was nearly ten.

"I'll just be gone a sec," she said, shouldering her purse.

When the door closed behind her, it was just me, the Paris night, and mental echoes of what Johanna had told me. I didn't know her parents, but I couldn't believe that after four years they wouldn't want her back in their lives. At the very least they would want to hear from her, know she was safe. But how much longer *would* she be safe? Despite Drake's assurances, Times Square was getting more dangerous, not less. And that scar on Johanna's arm had felt disturbingly like a knife wound. I needed to convince her to reach out to her parents.

When the door behind me cracked open, I turned, expecting to see Johanna. Instead, a lurid red mist entered the room. I stood and stumbled back toward the illusory window, colliding with the table en route. The drinks crashed to the floor. The mist gathered, morphing into the likeness of a woman of deadly beauty. With a grunt, I reached for my cane.

The foghorn alarm was sounding in my head now, indicating a breach. And the red was the same color as the energy I'd picked up at the crime scenes, meaning I'd found the perpetrator. Or rather, the perp had found me.

"Hello, darling," she purred.

My fingers closed around the cane, and I jerked it in front of me. *"Protezione!"* I shouted. But instead of creating a protective shield, the cane rattled in my hand like a sputtering motor, and the opal went dim.

The misty red being chuckled as she drifted nearer, her form taking even more sensual shape.

I tried again, but the power that moved through me was weaker than the last time and the cane sputtered out. *Huh?* I pulled my sword from the cane and, thrusting the blade toward the woman, shouted a force invocation. But nothing emanated from the beveled steel either.

"What's the matter, wizard?" she asked. "Can't work it up?"

The being's sultry voice coupled with the blatant sexuality blasting off her told me what she was. A succubus. They were quasi-demonic beings that seduced men in order to siphon out their souls. The epicenter of both of the victim's voids had been in the area of their groins, which made sense —that's where they would have been weakest following the, ahem, deed.

For a moment I thought the succubus was responsible for my loss of power, but then I remembered where I was. Certain types of fae magic could interfere with a magic-user's ability to cast. And this place was dripping with the stuff. No wonder the ogre doorman hadn't been concerned by my magical implements.

"Why the sour face?" the succubus asked. She was wearing an airy, low-cut gown that left almost nothing to the imagination. Even knowing what she was, I caught my body starting to respond.

"You see?" she purred. "I'm not so hard on the eyes."

I shook my head clear and began whispering every incantation I could to see if *anything* would move through me. With enough energy I could send her back to her realm. But the damned fae magic was mucking up my mental prism. My eyes flicked to the door. I considered running, but I didn't want her out in the club or the streets. I needed to end her here. The key was keeping her from arousing me until I could figure out exactly how to accomplish that.

I snorted. "You're not as attractive as you think you are."

"No?" she asked, her lush lips quirking in a way that almost knocked me over.

"No," I managed.

"But you do find me interesting, don't you? After all, you seem to follow me everywhere I go." Before I knew it, she was in front of me, running a fingernail in circles over my chest. "Now why is that, darling?"

When I tried to seize her hand to pull it away, my hand passed through mist.

"Is it that you want to get rid of me?" she asked, then *tsk*ed a few times. "I can't have that. I'm just starting to enjoy myself here."

The front of her body was pressed to mine now, and mist or not, I could feel every inch of her. My breath caught as she began moving up and down. Out in the club, I had felt pure bliss. This was pure lust. Though a part of my mind was screaming at me to get away, I didn't want her to stop.

The succubus was whispering in my ear now, ancient words meant to bind us sexually. When I felt the couch yield beneath me, I realized I was on my back. I was still dressed, but the succubus's gown had vanished—and she was straddling me. She began moving rhythmically.

It was too much, too nice…

If you don't get her off you in the next five seconds, you're going to end up like those other two—and with no one to help you.

I screwed my vision straight and made another attempt to push her away. Once more, my hand encountered nothing material. She might as well have been a ghost.

I stopped. *A ghost.*

I crept a hand into my coat pocket until I encountered my bag of salt. I dug out a handful and threw it in her face. In the instant the salt hit her, I saw her for the hideous being she was. Her face turned into a fanged skull, deep pits for eyes.

"Fucker!" she shouted as her misty form broke apart and whooshed from the room.

I thrashed upright and sat panting. Salt served multiple purposes in my line of work. I mainly carried it to neutralize magic or, in a pinch, to build a weak casting circle, but I'd also used it a few times to disperse pesky ghosts. I had been betting salt would have a similarly disruptive effect on the succubus. Thank God it had.

I dragged my hands through my hair. Seduced by a succubus. I felt like such a cliché.

But where in the hell had she come from? A being like that couldn't just drift around unattached. Once called up, she would need a host to remain on our plane. I was convinced now the host was Tabitha. I'd found her hair at both crime scenes, and according to Johanna, she had been coming to the club to meet us.

But what was she doing with a succubus in the first place? Had she intended for the succubus to kill those men? To kill me just now?

The door opened. This time it was Johanna.

"Change of plans," she said. "Tabitha's going to meet us at Tony's."

"Tony's?" I asked, fresh suspicion gnawing on me. "Why not here?"

"C'mon." As she walked over to take my hand, her gaze fell to the spilled drinks. "What happened?"

"I, ah, lost my balance."

"Is that salt on the couch?"

"Huh. I didn't even notice."

I could have told her about the succubus—she knew about enchantments and fae magic, after all—but her connection to Tabitha bothered me. The attack told me Tabitha had been in the club just now. Was Johanna covering for her? And if so, why? Ever since my trip to Romania, I'd developed a healthy skepticism toward mysterious women. I needed to figure out Johanna's role in this while avoiding any more fae magic. On the Parisian streetscape below, someone was giving a drunken toast.

"All right, let's go," I said.

Johanna and I left the VIP area and skirted the dance floor. As the ogre unbolted the door for us, I caught Johanna peering back, as if looking for someone. I followed her gaze, but no one seemed to be paying us any attention. Out in the street, power returned to my mental prism with a faint hum. My magic was coming back online. Johanna seemed more herself again too.

She wrapped her hands around my arm.

"So seriously, why the change of venue?" I asked.

"The club didn't feel safe."

Earlier, she'd implied that Tabitha was behind the change.

"Did you see someone?" I asked.

"I did, actual—" Her response broke off and became a scream. A force jerked her from my arms. In the same instant, a fist knocked my cane from my grasp. As it clattered off into the darkness, I spun to find the vampire Drake holding Johanna a foot off the ground by her throat.

"Put her down!" I shouted, rushing toward him.

Before I realized the vampire had moved, Drake's other hand met my chest. Stunned by the blow, I staggered back several steps and landed ass down on the sidewalk. I fought to draw my next breath.

"Time's up," he said.

"The hell are you talking about?" I wheezed. "That's not Tabitha."

Johanna's legs kicked fiercely while she wrestled with Drake's hands, but her struggles had no effect on the vampire. Above his sunglasses, his right eyebrow cocked up at me in question.

"Oh, no?"

"No," I managed, struggling to my feet. "Now put her down."

I hadn't gone more than a step when Drake reached into Johanna's purse and pulled something out. In the darkness, I couldn't see what. He tossed it to me. My first impression was that I'd just caught an animal. I juggled it in my hands before realizing what I was holding.

A red wig.

8

The blood drained from my face as I looked from the wig to Johanna.

"*Tabitha* is her street name," Drake said with a leering grin. "You were played by a whore."

Johanna grunted, the muscles on her forearms straining as she seized Drake's hand and fought to breathe. The enchanted knot bounced against the front of her blouse, but Drake had protection too. The large purple gem on his ring was counteracting the fae energy, which I realized was its function.

"Put her down," I insisted. "Let her talk."

"Every girl on the street is an actress, Everson, and this one is among the best I've seen. She's only going to tell you what you want to hear, and she'll make it sound oh so convincing. You've already said it yourself—*she's* the connection to the victims. *She's* the one behind the attacks."

I'd been duped before, but I refused to believe Johanna had just tried to kill me.

"She's fire, Everson," he continued. "Keep playing with her, and you're going to get incinerated."

I opened my wizard senses. If Johanna was harboring the succubus, I would see it. But with fae magic still polluting my system, I was greeted with flashing afterimages of pink and blue lights. There *had* to be an explanation for the wig, and Johanna was the only one who could provide it, actress or not. When I switched back to my normal vision, she remained suspended in Drake's grasp.

"Down," I said, pushing power through the word.

My wizard's voice typically only worked on the weak-minded and impressionable—and vampires were rarely either—but without my sword and staff, it was one of the only weapons left to me.

When Drake's lips pressed together, I thought he was going to snap Johanna's neck. With his vampire strength, it would have taken almost no effort. But he lowered her, switching his grip to her upper arm. Johanna coughed and wiped her eyes. I didn't know if my wizard's voice had compelled Drake, but it might have tipped the scales just enough.

"This should be entertaining," the vampire said.

I stepped forward but stopped short of touching Johanna, even though I wanted to make sure she was okay.

"So you're Tabitha," I said.

I wasn't asking. I knew. It explained Johanna's interest in *my* interest in Tabitha last night. It explained her evasiveness around my questions into Tabitha's whereabouts. It explained why none of my spells had worked on the hairs—they were synthetic, not organic. And when I thought back to my call to Tabitha earlier, I could hear Johanna's voice in the recording now.

She finished coughing and raised her face. It was tear-streaked and pleading. I wanted to pull her from Drake's grasp and take her somewhere safe. But first I needed some good answers.

"I was..." She paused to cough again. "I was going to tell you tonight. I wanted to know what you wanted with her. Had to make sure you weren't going to hurt her ... Hurt me."

"Oh, you poor thing," Drake laughed.

"You were going to tell me in there?" I asked.

I was trying to think like a succubus. If the being *were* attached to Johanna, this would have been the ideal place to strike—a fae club where I would be rendered powerless. Was it any coincidence the succubus had appeared right after Johanna stepped out to use the restroom? Thanks to my salt, the attack had failed. The succubus had fled back to her host, but before the entity could reconstitute herself and make another grab for my soul, Johanna must have spotted Drake in the club. That's why she had been in such a hurry for us to leave.

"It was the safest place I could think of," she said.

A reasonable answer, given the neighborhood, but it didn't put my suspicions to bed. I had little doubt the succubus was using her as a host. The question was whether Johanna was a pawn or a willing participant. Even before the succubus's attack, Johanna had been enticing me in her own mortal way.

I decided to go direct.

"How long have you been possessed?"

"Possessed?" Her eyes searched mine. "What are you talking about?" She appeared at an honest loss, but with Drake's actress line still pinging around my head, I refused to believe her.

"Don't bullshit me."

"I'm not, Everson," she said firmly.

"You took a client to the Lincoln hotel last night, right? A big guy name Al?"

"What about him?"

"Why was part of his soul missing?"

"His soul?"

"And what about the man you entertained tonight in the parking lot? James?"

She was having trouble holding my gaze, but whether from guilt or shame, I couldn't tell.

"Did you know a chunk of his soul is gone too?" I asked, anger hardening my voice.

"I don't know what you're talking about. I didn't *attack* anyone. I've never *attacked* anyone." The anger in her own voice surprised me, but was it part of the act? "And I'm not fucking possessed."

She tried to shake herself loose from Drake, but he kept a firm hold on her. He appeared to be enjoying the back and forth.

"I told you she'd sound convincing," he said. He canted his head toward Johanna and cinched his grip, making her grimace. "But now for some honesty," he said. "How do you explain your ability to work alone out here for … How long has it been? Four years now?"

I almost told Drake to back off, but I wanted an answer too.

"I have friends," she grunted.

"Do you mean that half-fae whore? Or is it the little runt who can barely see above a steering wheel?" His face hardened as he twisted her arm behind her back. She fell to her knees with a cry.

I stepped forward. "That's enough."

"I was willing to tolerate you putting ideas into my girls'

heads that I have to snuff out like damned fires," he continued. "But when you start going after the clientele, you've crossed a line."

When he twisted again, Johanna's scream lanced my heart.

"That's enough, I said!"

But I could see in the vampire's face that he meant to finish her. I looked wildly around for my cane, but I couldn't spot it. When I turned back to Johanna, her forehead was to the sidewalk, her arm angled behind her back, on the verge of snapping. Drake seized her neck with his other hand. Beyond Johanna's curtain of hair, the fae knot glowed futilely. I focused on the silvery charm. By itself, the charm and Drake's ring were at a stalemate.

But with some extra juice...

"Attivare!" I shouted.

The protective power in the knot contracted for an instant before exploding out in a violent pulse, shattering the purple gem on Drake's ring. The vampire screamed as the fiery white blast pummeled into him. Blown from Johanna, he slapped frantically at the flames bursting over his body.

"Come on," I said, grasping Johanna's hand.

She stood, and we began to run. In the white firelight, I saw my cane in the gutter. I veered over to pick it up. As we hurried toward Broadway, I cast a shield around us. Before turning the corner, I peeked back. Drake had fallen to his knees as the fiery white magic claimed him. Though vampires weren't my responsibility, one less bloodsucker was never a bad thing.

"You're a wizard," Johanna panted, "aren't you?" There was no sense trying to hide it. She'd heard my invocation and seen the results. But before I could answer, she continued.

"Everson, I swear ... I'm not possessed."

I looked into her eyes. I wanted to believe her, but it went against all of the evidence.

"Is there somewhere private we can go?" I asked.

She nodded. "My place."

9

Johanna's place was in Chelsea, just north of my own apartment in the West Village. We rode there in a cab, the gulf between us feeling much larger than the two feet of backseat that separated us. I didn't trust her, and she knew it. For the entire ride, neither of us spoke. I kept one hand in my bag of salt in case the succubus decided to try her luck again.

When the cab pulled in front of the apartment building, there was something familiar about it. And then it hit me. I'd been called to the address just a couple of weeks earlier. When I'd arrived, though, the alarm had stopped and my hunting spell had died. The citywide wards sometimes misfired—something Chicory kept promising to fix—and I assumed that had been the case then.

But now I suspected the alarm had detected the succubus first being called up.

I reinforced the shield around myself as I followed Johanna into the building. We climbed several flights and emerged onto a hallway. Pulling a set of keys from her purse, she stopped at the first door.

"There's no one here," she said, unlocking the door and pushing it open, "but you're welcome to search the place if it'll make you feel better."

I followed her into a living room that featured an eclectic mix of furniture and a modest entertainment center. To the right was a kitchen, and to the left a corridor that led to the bedrooms. Johanna set her purse on a table by the door. I examined her neck where the vampire had grabbed her, but I couldn't see any lasting marks.

"I need you to do something," I said.

"Sure, what?"

I took a chair from the kitchen and placed it in the center of the living room. "Sit here and don't ask any questions."

I was surprised by how readily she complied. Without saying anything, I took the tube of copper filings from my pocket and sprinkled what remained into a circle around her. I could feel her watching me. When I finished, I stood back and spoke a soft incantation. The circle glowed with power, hardening the air around her. She and the succubus were now trapped.

"I'll be right back."

I left her, and went through each room of the apartment. Jade's room was easy to identify with its fae-like colors and various charms. Among her books were several on casting. The next room must have been Candy's. Stuffed animals crowded the bed while the walls were lined with posters of hip hop artists and shirtless hunks. At last, I came to Johanna's room.

Something told me I could have been standing in her childhood bedroom. The twin bed with a yellow home-stitched comforter. The wooden desk. The bookshelf with titles of classic literature and a row of second-hand textbooks on anthropology: the courses Johanna hadn't been able to take. In a box under her bed, I found a framed photo of her between a smiling man and woman I assumed to be her parents. Their smiles appeared forced, while the teenaged Johanna wasn't smiling at all. Further down were a clutch of medals for ballet competitions.

I returned to the living room, satisfied the apartment was clear.

"The others won't be home for hours," Johanna said, as if to reassure me. I could see by her eyes that by putting herself at my mercy she was hoping to regain my trust. I stood in front of her.

"I believe what you told me," I said.

"You do?"

Her bedroom lined up with her story, the photo especially, and I didn't believe her acting extended that far. "But here's the thing," I said. "I still think you're possessed. You just don't know it."

I could see by her set jaw she wasn't convinced, but she shrugged a shoulder. "Then do whatever you have to do to know one way or the other. Short of killing me," she added.

There were two ways to destroy a succubus. The first, and easier, method *was* to behead the host. The second was to remove the being from the host and then disperse it with a high dose of energy.

"That won't be necessary," I said. "But first I need to ask you some questions."

"Shoot."

"That scar on your arm. How did it happen?"

She looked down at her shoulder and tugged on the sleeve, even though the scar was already hidden. "Someone got to me."

"A client?"

She looked away. "Yeah, a regular. He'd never tried to hurt

me before. He'd always been really respectful. But that night, he pulled a knife and gashed my arm. Started sucking the blood like he was starving."

I nodded. Sounded like a man who had been vampire-attacked.

"It took awhile for this to work," Johanna said, touching the fae knot around her neck. "It eventually forced him off me, but I needed eighteen stitches and two pints of O-negative to put me back together. Jade strengthened the charm, but ... if it had taken another minute to kick in—or if it hadn't kicked in at all—I wouldn't be here talking to you."

I could guess where this was going. "So what did you do?" I prompted.

"When I first started renting here, one of the conditions was that I never go into Jade's room or touch her books. After a month, curiosity got the better of me, and I looked through one of her spell books. Strange stuff, but I remembered there being a spell in there having to do with a guardian, a being of protection. After the attack, I thought about that spell. A lot. I hadn't worked in two weeks, and the idea of going back to Times Square made me shake all over. If I could have a guardian like that, you know for insurance..."

Bingo.

"So, I followed the directions," she said, "and, well, nothing happened."

"Nothing?" I looked at her. "Are you sure?"

"There was this red mist, but it broke apart. Other than that?" She shook her head. "No guardian appeared, and nothing possessed me or turned me into a monster, as you seem to think."

"So why did you go back to work?"

"Necessity. I was getting low on money."

I nodded. I had enough information. As an amateur

conjurer, Johanna wouldn't have been able to call up a guardian. That was an advanced spell few magic-users, present company included, could have managed. But her energy *had* attracted the attention of a succubus spirit, maybe because of her occupation. That's what Johanna had called up, red mist and all.

"What I'm about to do won't hurt," I said. "But it won't be pleasant."

"Do your worst," Johanna said with a small smirk, but I sensed her fear.

A succubus tended to stick with one host, integrating with that host's makeup—not unlike how Thelonious had attached himself to me. But because a succubus wasn't a true demon, exorcism wouldn't work. The task, then, was to make the succubus as uncomfortable in Johanna's skin as possible. Once the succubus left in search of a new host, I could trap and hit the being with a dispersive bolt of energy, sending her back to her realm for good.

Reaching into a coat pocket, I pulled out a bag of grumby roots and scattered them inside the circle around Johanna's feet. I stood back and spoke an invocation. The roots crackled and began to emit a noxious smoke.

"I need you to breathe it in."

Johanna's nose wrinkled, but she did as I said. I watched closely for signs that the succubus was getting irritated. That usually manifested in the host as tremors and writhing, as well as a sudden ability to speak in tongues. But after a minute of Johanna coughing, I didn't witness any of that.

"I can barely breathe," she called through the column of smoke.

Was I dealing with a really stubborn succubus? Or was Johanna right about not being possessed?

"Everson?" she pled.

"Dammit," I muttered.

With a Word, I dispersed the circle. The smoke blew away from Johanna along with the scattering magic. She remained stooped over, coughing into a fist. I hurried into the kitchen and poured a glass of water. By the time I came back, her coughing was coming under control.

She accepted the glass and took a sip. "I'd be lying if I said tonight was going how I'd pictured it," she said weakly.

"Heh. That makes two of us."

I was thinking about my failed bid to force the succubus from her body. What if the succubus hadn't possessed Johanna, but one of her roommates? Jade had seemed a little too vigilant both times I'd seen her. She could have followed me to the club and waited until I was alone.

"Was there anyone else here the day you cast the spell?" I asked.

"Let's see ... Jade was out, otherwise I wouldn't have borrowed her book..."

All right, scratch Jade, I thought.

"But Candy was here," Johanna said suddenly. "She had this terrible cold. Spent the whole day in bed." She stopped. "You don't think...?"

Sick and sleeping would have been like setting out a welcome mat for a succubus. And Candy had taken me to the club. She'd known where I was, where I could be attacked. I had seen her leave, but she could easily have turned around and come back after I'd entered.

At that moment, the foghorn sounded in my head. Another alarm.

Fresh out of copper filings, I used my bag of salt to sprinkle out another circle to cast a hunting spell. Minutes later, the cane kicked in my hands and spun me north. Something told me the damned succubus was loose again and that I was headed back to Times Square.

I rose and turned to Johanna. "I've gotta go."

"I'm coming with you," she said, already reading the situation. "Candy's like a sister. Besides, I'll know where to find her."

10

Johanna and I got out of the cab near the corner of Broadway and Forty-fourth. The hunting spell had been petering out, which suggested the succubus had returned to her host and I was only picking up remnants of her presence. I stood on the sidewalk a moment until the cane gave another feeble tug. It was pulling me toward the alley that ran behind Tony's diner.

"Stay here," I told Johanna.

"Be careful," she called after me.

I crept down the alleyway until I was past the Dumpster I'd cast behind earlier. I could see the remnants of my casting circle, but now there were two sprawled bodies—the junkies I'd had to step over. The spiraling voids where parts of their souls had once been carried the succubus's mark. Junkies would not have been her first choice for a meal, but weakened by my attack, she'd had to look for low-hanging prey.

I scanned the alleyway before enclosing the junkies in cocoons of gauzy light and returning to where Johanna was standing. "I am so sorry for putting you through the ringer at your apartment," I said, hugging her. "Not only do I believe you, but you're not possessed."

"But I *am* Tabitha. You had a right to be suspicious."

I kissed her cheek and rubbed her arms. "When this is over, I owe you dinner."

"I could go for a steak. But what's the plan?"

"You said you knew where to find Candy?"

"Yeah."

I looked down the alleyway and thought for a moment. I felt the bags of salt and grumby root in my pocket. I would have just enough. "All right," I said, turning back to her. "We're going to set a little trap."

A HALF HOUR LATER, I was crouched behind the Dumpster, my hairline damp with sweat. Johanna had been gone too long. Did the succubus know we were onto her? Had sending Johanna out alone been a mistake?

I was debating whether or not to go in search of her when a pair of silhouettes appeared at the entrance to the alley. My pulse quickened. It was Johanna, and Candy was with her.

I could hear them talking, but I couldn't make out what they were saying. Johanna started down the alleyway. After some hesitation, Candy followed.

I'd set up the salt circle about a quarter of the way down, scattered it with grumby root, and disguised the arrangement with old newspapers. The second Candy stepped into it, Johanna would give me a signal. I'd close the circle and have my succubus. Then it was a matter of activating the root, driving the being out of Candy's body, and blasting it from our realm.

Candy stopped, and I could hear her telling Johanna she was scared to go any farther.

C'mon, just a few more steps, I thought.

Johanna returned to her side and took her arm. With gentle words, she coaxed her roommate into continuing. I could see Johanna watching the ground. When they reached the circle, she separated from Candy and brushed back her hair with her right hand: the signal.

"Cerrare!" I shouted, closing the circle.

Candy screamed as the air hardened around her.

I sprang from my hiding place and activated the root. As the column filled with smoke, Johanna reassured Candy. "It's not going hurt," she said. "It's to purge something from your system."

"It stinks!" Candy shouted.

"Just try to breathe normally," Johanna told her.

"I..." Candy fell into a fit of coughing. "I can't!"

As I approached, Johanna turned to me with worried eyes. "Are you sure?"

"Who else could it be?"

We were both watching the column for the release of red mist from Candy's body when footsteps sounded behind us. I turned. At the far end of the alleyway, a heavyset figure had appeared from behind the stacked pallets and was striding toward us. I pulled my sword from my staff.

"Who in the hell is that?" I asked.

I wasn't expecting an answer, so was surprised when Johanna said. "That's my fricking social worker. Barbara."

"Your social worker?"

"She was in the fae club earlier. That's why I left."

"I thought you left because you'd seen Drake."

Johanna shook her head. "Barbara has always taken an

interest in my case, but recently she gained all this weight and started acting super stalkerish."

Recently...

"She wasn't there the day you cast the spell, was she?"

Johanna started to shake her head again, then stopped. "Wait, yeah. Yeah, she was. We had a scheduled visit I'd forgotten all about. Right after the mist appeared, she arrived at the apartment to check on me."

Crap, so the succubus hadn't gone after Candy. For whatever reason, it had made a host of the frigging social worker. I eyed the late middle-aged woman as her flats beat toward us. She was dressed conservatively, slacks and a plaid jacket. Her frosted hair stood in a short, stiff column. For a second, I doubted she was the host, but then the woman's eyes began to glow red.

Yeah, succubus central.

With a Word, I dispersed Candy's confinement. She emerged, gagging, from the cylinder of smoke. "Take her and get out of here," I said to Johanna. "Now!" I shouted when she hesitated.

I moved toward Barbara, adjusting my grip on sword and staff.

"Did I surprise you, darling?" she asked in the succubus's voice.

"You could say that."

"Don't let the package fool you. This woman has sex on her brain 24-7, making her the perfect host."

"Why not Johanna or Candy?" I asked.

I was trying to buy time to think. I wasn't going to decapitate the social worker. She was an innocent victim. No, I needed to flush out the entity. Problem was I'd used all of my salt to create the casting circle. I peeked over. Except for a small scuff, the circle was still intact. If I could lure the succubus into the circle and close it, I could activate the remaining root.

"Those girls dance around the act," the succubus said in response to my question, "but they're not into it. This woman, however..." She released a husky laugh. "You'd turn seven shades of red if I told you the things that run through her mind. Not only that, she had a professional relationship with your friend. When the hunger for a male soul struck, I had only to follow Johanna discreetly. Once she finished, I would park my host and move in. In the males' spent states, they were far too weak to resist me. The consumption was effortless, making it that much more tasty." She actually licked her lips. "After centuries of seducing, it's nice to have someone else do the heavy lifting for a change."

"I'll bet," I muttered, stepping around the circle.

"But then you came along, wizard, threatening to fuck up my meal ticket."

"Yeah, I have a bad habit of doing that."

"Why is it your concern, anyway? I only take enough to fill, not kill." She patted her belly. "And I never return to the same man twice. I have adventurous tastes, if you catch me."

"I think you're biting off a lot more soul than you realize."

I continued to back away, the circle now between us. In another ten feet, she'd be standing inside it.

"I'm not upset, though," she went on. "Far from it. After all, I would never have met you otherwise. Let's just say I've become a little obsessed. It's not every day a girl gets a taste of wizard essence."

"I'm sorry the obsession isn't mutual."

"That's the beauty of being a connoisseur of souls," she said, her eyes glinting. "It doesn't have to be."

When she stepped into the circle, I lunged forward and smoothed the scuff with a shoe. But before I could speak the invocation to close the circle, she landed a lightning-fast blow to my chin. I staggered back, the connection to my legs failing. The alleyway tilted in my vision. It wasn't until I hit the ground that I realized I'd dropped my sword and staff.

"I watched you set the trap earlier, silly. Did you think I would fall for it too?" She swept the circle apart with a shoe, crossed it, and then lowered herself until she was gazing into my eyes. "Now, where were we?"

Barbara's features began to morph until I was looking at the sensual creature who'd surprised me at the club. Before I knew it, she was kissing me. The alleyway swooned again as a flood of pleasure hormones dumped into my brain. I felt the back of my head thud against the asphalt.

Seduced twice by the same succubus? a distant part of me asked in disbelief.

The creature smiled lasciviously as she mounted my hips. "Having to do the heavy lifting isn't always a bad thing," she said, her words a long, dark caress. "Just relax, wizard, and enjoy the ride."

Only I was the one about to get ridden.

I screwed up my eyes, but I couldn't see through the illusion to the social worker. And the illusion was so damned jaw-dropping. I stretched out a hand along the asphalt until my fingers encountered the grit of salt. I managed to gather a pinch and flick it at her.

Her throaty laugh was as intoxicating as the rest of her. "Not this time, darling. I'm safely inside my flesh package." She leaned down until our lips were just brushing. "Now let go," she breathed. "When you wake up, you'll remember this as the most amazing dream you've ever had. Is that so awful?"

When her tongue grabbed mine, I felt something unlatch in my groin. Not on a physical level, but deeper. My soul was coming unmoored. I could feel the succubus's greed. She called herself a connoisseur, but she was a glutton in denial. The lion's share of my soul was about to get sucked out. There wasn't going to be any waking up or dream-remembering.

I can think of worse ways to go, I thought dimly.

But a part of me regretted not being able to take Johanna out to dinner like I'd promised. I'd wanted to convince her to call her parents, to leave the city before something like this happened to her. As the thought drowned beneath a tsunami of pleasure, I thought I saw Johanna. And she was wielding a two-by-four.

"Eat wood, bitch," she grunted.

The plank smashed into the succubus's head, knocking her off me. I shoved myself backwards as my strength and willpower flooded back in. Barbara turned toward Johanna with fiery eyes, blood shining over her right temple.

"I called you up," Johanna shouted. "Now I command you to go away!"

The succubus grinned and extended a hand of writhing fingers. "If only it were that easy."

Before I could do anything, a misty red blast shot from her palm and slammed into Johanna. The protective knot Johanna wore glowed silver, but it was too little too late. She collapsed to the ground, the two by four clanking down beside her. I felt the succubus train her attention back on me.

"Sorry for the interruption, darling," she purred.

When I turned, I saw where she'd fallen. The salt circle was destroyed, but grumby root remained scattered beneath her. I snatched up my staff and shouted, *"Protezione!"*

The succubus's head whipped around as a light dome enclosed her. With a second invocation, I ignited the roots. Noxious smoke billowed around her. I retrieved my sword and gained my feet.

From inside the dome-shaped shield, the social worker

thrashed and shouted in garbled tongues. *That* had been the reaction I'd been looking for earlier. But while a shield would contain the host, I would need a casting circle to contain the succubus when she was forced out.

I ran forward and, using a shoe, began shoving the scattered salt into a semblance of a circle. In my peripheral vision, I could see the orange kitten peering out at the spectacle from behind the Dumpster.

With a final scream, the social worker reared her head back. A violent torrent of red mist poured from her open mouth. Shit. The entity swirled above the shield in a red storm, as though orienting herself, gathering strength, and then shot toward Johanna, who was still down.

"*Vigore!*" I shouted, aiming my sword into the path of the succubus.

The force blast caught the entity and sent her careening toward the kitten. Needing a life force, *any* life force, the succubus funneled into the mewling creature.

"*Cerrare!*" I shouted, locking the succubus inside the thrashing kitten.

Possessed now, the kitten tried to dash behind the Dumpster. I pulled it out with a force invocation and pinned it in front of me. I raised my blade. Decapitation would end the succubus threat once and for all.

But as I eyed the scrawny little critter with its ochre green eyes, I hesitated, then lowered the blade.

I couldn't do it. Not like this.

I reached into a coat pocket and pulled out a dropper bottle that contained a sleeping potion. A single drop on the kitten's tongue, and it was out like a light. I lifted the little thing—it couldn't have weighed more than a pound—and set it gently into an empty coat pocket. I would banish the succubus back at my lab.

I turned to where Johanna had fallen and found her sitting up.

"Thank God," I breathed, rushing to her side. "Are you all right?"

She nodded groggily. "Whatever she hit me with put me to sleep. Is she gone?"

"Pretty much." With an arm around her waist, I helped her up and waited until she felt steady on her feet. "C'mon, let's get you home."

11

One week later

"Well, Everson," Johanna said, as I signed the check. "Congrats on being the best date I've had since I've been in New York."

After everything she had been through, including having to save my butt, an upscale steak house was the least I could do. We'd both ordered the New York strip, and they'd been excellent. "Hey, date's not over yet," I said.

"No?" she arched an eyebrow.

"No, meaning I still have time to mess it up."

She laughed and took a sip of her wine. I was enjoying watching her enjoy herself. She had gotten her hair done and worn a beautiful black evening gown for our night out. I felt a little guilty in my pedestrian shirt and blazer. As she set her glass down, you would never have guessed she worked in Times Square. And that's what I needed to talk to her about.

"Listen," I said, pushing my to-go box to one side. "Have you given any more thought to what I brought up last week?"

"You mean about calling my parents?"

I nodded, feeling more like her guidance counselor than her date.

"Already done," she said. "Last night."

"Really?"

"When the line started ringing, I honestly thought I was going to be sick. I came this close to hanging up. And then my dad answered."

"What did he say?" I asked, my own heart pounding.

"Nothing at first. I said, 'Hi, Daddy,' and he started crying. I'd never heard him cry before. So of course I started crying too." She rolled her eyes. "When we finally got control of ourselves, he thanked God that I was all right. He said that he and my mother had been thinking about me ever since I left. Here I'd been expecting the malice I'd heard the day I pulled out of their driveway, but he sounded like a big Teddy bear. He got my mom, and the three of us talked until midnight. I told them everything that had happened—leaving out details about my work, of course. But it was really good, Everson. Really clearing. You were right. I should have done it a long time ago. I feel awful for what I put them through."

"That's incredible," I said.

"They even offered to pay for me to go back to school. I accepted, but I'm not going to do it here. I've decided to move back to my hometown. It's the least I owe them. There's a state school nearby with a good anthro program."

"And no talk of ballet?" I asked.

She waved a hand. "I'm almost twenty-four now, which is considered ancient in that world. I'm sure that helped, too."

"Well, I'm happy for you."

"And I have you to thank. And the succubus."

I tilted my head in surprise. "The succubus? Why her?"

"When she knocked me out with that red mist, I fell into a kind of dream state. Though it was more like a nightmare. I was trapped in this writhing mass of naked bodies, and no matter which direction I struggled, I couldn't get out. That's how my life here felt. And that's when everything became clear: in leaving home, I only ended up trading one prison for another." Her eyes glistened. "The night you walked into Tony's and I heard you ask about Tabitha, I had this strange feeling you were going to be my ticket out. I didn't know how, but a week later, and listen to me. My social worker must have told me to call my parents a hundred times, but coming from you, someone I ... well, I respect ... it was different."

I took her hands in mine, thinking about what I would have given to have known my own parents. "I'm glad I could help, Johanna. How is your social worker, by the way?" Johanna had called Jade the night of the attack and asked her to recover Barbara from the alleyway. Apparently, Jade found her stumbling around in a daze.

"She took the week off, but otherwise, fine," Johanna answered.

"And Candy?" I asked.

"I convinced her to move down with me. Fresh start."

"That's great. Tell her I'm sorry about fumigating her."

Johanna giggled. "I will. Since we're giving updates on everyone, how's the succubus? Banished, I presume?"

"Well..."

She leaned forward and whispered, *"What?"*

"Here's the thing. When I got the kitten back to my lab—it's a she, by the way—the succubus was so tangled up in her soul that I couldn't extract her. Not without doing serious damage to the kitten." Hell, I wasn't sure the succubus could even extract herself. The locking spell I'd cast on her was meant for objects, not spirits.

"So what are you going to do?" Johanna asked.

"Keep her, I guess. Act as her warden."

"And you'll be safe?"

"Well, I'm taking precautions. I've already warded the apartment, and—" I stopped suddenly and laughed. "Can I just say that being able to talk to someone about this stuff is the most amazing thing ever. I'm so happy you're going home, but at the same time I'm kind of bummed."

She reached across the table, brushed my cheek with the backs of her fingers, and kissed me softly. "You can always visit."

"True enough," I said. Could I, though? What would happen if a creature popped into the city and I was five hundred miles away? I didn't exactly have backup. Besides, Johanna needed a clean break from New York.

"In the meantime, you have ... What's your kitten's name?"

"Haven't given her one yet," I said. "Kitty?"

"Tabitha," Johanna declared. "Something to remember our little adventure by."

"Tabitha it is, then."

12

I returned to my apartment late that night and unlocked the three bolts. I checked the wards to make sure nothing had gotten in—or out—and shut and locked the door behind me. As I turned up the lights in the large space, it didn't seem so empty. Probably because I still hadn't come down from my date.

Plus, I had a housemate now.

"Kitty?" I called. "I mean, Tabitha?"

I couldn't see her, but I noticed that the bottoms of my curtains had been torn to shreds. In the kitchen, I set the to-go box with my leftover steak on the counter and pulled a bottle of goat's milk from the fridge. She'd been refusing to eat, so I was trying anything I could think of. While the milk warmed in a pot on the stove, I cut up the medium-rare steak on a plate. When the milk began to steam, I poured it into a bowl and carried plate and bowl into the living room.

"Tabitha?" I called again.

I set the food beside a short divan I barely used and stood back.

Seconds later, a small orange face appeared from behind the couch. Her green eyes darted between me and the food. I bit back a smile, reminding myself that the adorable little critter was still possessed by a succubus.

"I brought you some din-din," I sang.

She made a sound that sounded suspiciously like *fuck you* before trotting over to the steak. In a storm of chomping she took the steak down and then trained her hunger on the steaming milk.

Finally, I thought. *Something she likes. Just as long as she doesn't become too attached. Stuff's not cheap.*

The succubus-kitten finished the milk in surprisingly quick time. Then, licking her lips, she hopped up onto the divan and collapsed onto her side, her belly a perfectly round sphere. I waited until she was snoring before walking over and standing above her. She looked so innocent, her mouth partway open, one paw curled behind her ear. We just needed to put some weight on her.

"Sleep tight, little Tabitha," I whispered.

Twenty minutes later I climbed into bed, already missing Johanna but strangely content that I had company in the next room. I wasn't naïve. Successfully cohabitating with a succubus was going to take time. I would have to evaluate the situation on a constant basis, remaining ever vigilant.

But as I lay there, fingers laced behind my head, thoughts starting to drift, I couldn't help but ponder what the future might hold for me and my new cat.

Uneasy roommates? Reluctant confidants? Work partners? Friends? I checked to ensure the wards over my bedroom door were at full strength before closing my eyes.

The only certainty was that life here was going to get much more interesting.

THE END

But be sure to catch up with Everson Croft in his first full-length novel, Demon Moon. *Keep reading for a preview...*

DEMON MOON

A PREVIEW OF PROF CROFT BOOK 1

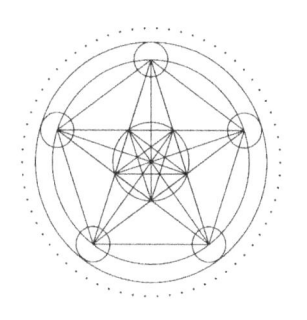

1

I blew out a curse as the first cold droplets of rain pelted my face and punched through my magic. As if I wasn't already running late.

Making an umbrella of my coat collar, I stooped into a run, skirting bags of garbage that swelled from the fronts of row houses like pustules, but it was no use. The downpour that blackened the sidewalk and drove rats from the festering piles also broke apart my hunting spell.

And it had been one of my better ones.

I took refuge on a crumbling porch and shook out my coat. I was in the pit of the East Village, and it stunk. Except for a flicker of street light, the block was midnight dark, the building across the way a brick shell, hollowed out by arson. Not the domicile of the conjurer I needed to stop. Or more likely save.

Assuming I could find him now.

"*Seguire,*" I said in a low, thrumming voice.

Most hunting spells worked like a dowsing rod, pulling the user toward the source of something. In this case, taboo magic. But reliable hunting spells, such as those needed to navigate New York's convoluted streets, required time to prepare. And even then they were delicate.

"*Seguire,*" I repeated, louder.

Though the storm was already sweeping off, the spell refused to take shape again. I swore under my breath. Magic and moving water made poor bedfellows. And here I'd dropped a fat hundred on the booster: ground narwhal tusk. Sunk cost, I thought bitterly as I hustled back to the sidewalk. There were a lot of those in wizardry, my svelte wallet the proof.

Splashing in the direction I'd been pulled before the cloudburst, I gave up on the hunting spell and resorted to twenty-twenty vision, scanning passing buildings for signs of life.

As the sidewalks thickened with larger mounds of garbage, the rats became more territorial. I knocked aside several with my walking cane. The soul eaters that hunkered like shadows in the below-ground stairwells weren't quite so bold. They watched with hollow eyes before shrinking from the protective power of my necklace, in search of weaker, drug-addled prey. Luckily for them, post-Crash New York was a boomtown for chemical addiction.

Unfortunately for me, the financial crash had also made a growth stock of amateur conjurers.

They tended to be men and women seeking lost money or means—or simply some meaning where their prior faith, whether spiritual or material, seemed to have failed them. Understandable, certainly, but as far as my work went, a royal pain in the ass. Most mortals could only access the nether realms, and shallowly at that. In their fat-fingered efforts, they called up grubby creatures better left undisturbed. Ones more inclined to make a sopping meal of a conjurer's heart than grant his material wishes.

Trust me, it wasn't pretty.

Neither was the job of casting the charming beings back to their realms, but it was the job I'd been decreed. I had some nice acid burns and a missing right ear lobe to prove it. A business card might have read:

Everson Croft
Wizard Garbage Collector

Nice, huh? But unlike the city's striking sanitation workers, I couldn't just walk off the job.

Small messes became big messes, and in magical terms, that was a recipe for ruin. The apocalyptic kind. Better to scoop up the filth, drop it down the hatch, and batten down the lid. Plenty of ancient evils lurked in the Deep Down, their senses attuned to the smallest openings to our world. Human history was dotted with near misses, thanks in part to the vigilance of my lineage.

The thought of being the one to screw up that streak was hell on a good night's sleep, let me tell you.

At Avenue C, I rounded a small mountain of plowed trash and shuffled to a stop. A new scent was skewering the vaporous reek, hooking like a talon in my throat. A sickly-sweet scent, like crushed cockroach or…

Fear spread through me as I raised my eyes toward the source: a steep apartment building with a pair of lights burning near the top floor. Dark magic dissipated above the building in a blood-red haze.

I *was* too late. And whatever the conjurer had summoned was no cockroach.

"Crap," I spat, and launched into a run.

The smell was distinctly demonic.

2
———

I stumbled into a blacked-out lobby, raised my ironwood cane, and uttered, *"Illuminare."*

White light swelled from an opal inset in the cane's end to reveal an upended concierge's desk and graffiti-smeared walls. The single elevator door opposite me was open. I moved toward it, noting the message sprayed over the burned-out elevator lights: "STEP RIGHT IN," with an arrow inviting riders into a carless shaft. I peeked down the two-story plunge to a subbasement, where I could hear something large thump-dragging around.

No thanks.

I hit the stairwell and took the steps two at a time. The cloying smell from the street sharpened in my sinuses, making my eyes water. I had smelled demon before, but in Eastern Europe, years ago—the near-death experience had marked my passage into wizardhood, in a way.

But no, never here. Not in New York.

Which meant a seriously evil conjurer had slipped under the Order's watchful gaze. I considered sending up a message, but that would take energy I couldn't afford at the moment—

not to mention time. The Oracular Order of Magi and Magical Beings was an esteemed and ancient body. Accordingly, they made decisions at a pace on par with the Mendenhall glacier.

That, and I was still on their iffy list for what had happened ten years earlier, during the aforementioned demonic encounter. Never mind that my actions (which, okay, *had* involved summoning an incubus spirit) saved my life, or that I was only twenty-two at the time.

So yeah, the less contact with the Order, the better, I'd since learned.

Between the third and fourth floors, the stairwell began to vibrate. At the fifth floor—the one on which I'd observed the lights from outside—the vibrating became a hammering. I pulled the stairwell door open onto a stink of hard diesel and understood the commotion's source: a gas-powered generator. At the hallway's end, light outlined a door.

I was halfway to the door when a woman's scream pierced the tumult. Jerking my cane into two parts, I gripped a staff in my left hand and a steel sword in my right. A shadow grew around the door a second before it banged open.

The man was six foot ten, easy. Blades of black tattooing scaled his pin-pierced face, giving over to an all-out ink fight on his shaved scalp. Leather and spiked studs stretched over powerful arms holding what looked like a pump-action shotgun.

The sorcerer's bodyguard?

He inclined forward, squinting into the dim hallway. The screaming behind him continued, accompanied now by angry beats and the wail of a guitar. I exhaled and sheathed my sword.

Punks. The literal kind.

"Hey!" Tattoo Face boomed as I retreated back toward the

stairwell. "You're missing a kickass set. Blade's only on till two." Then as a further inducement: "Half cover, since you got here late."

I sniffed the air, but the generator's fumes were still clouding over the demon smell. I couldn't fix on a direction. I returned to Tattoo Face, shouting to be heard. "Do you live here?"

He shrugged as he lowered the shotgun. "Live. Squat."

"Seen anyone strange in the building?" I peered past him into the hazy room of head-bangers, the pink-haired singer/screamer—Blade, I presumed—standing on the hearth of a bricked-over fireplace. I decided to rephrase the question. "Anyone who looks like they don't belong?"

Behind all of his ink, the punk's face was surprisingly soft, almost boyish, but it hardened as I stepped more fully into the generator-powered light. I followed his gaze down to where my tweed jacket and dark knit tie peeked from the parting flaps of my trench coat. Beneath his own jacket, he was wearing a bandolier of shotgun shells.

"You a narc or something?" he asked.

I shook my head. "Just looking for someone."

His eyes fell further to my walking cane, which, not to polish my own brass, was at definite odds with someone six feet tall and in his apparent prime. My hairline had receded slightly, but still... Tattoo Face frowned studiously, as though still undecided if he could trust me.

"I help people," I added.

After another moment, he nodded. "Strange guy showed up a couple of weeks ago. Hauled a big trunk upstairs." He raised his eyes. "Unit right above ours. Talks to himself. Same things, over and over."

I sprinted back to the stairwell, not bothering with the

usual pretense of a trick knee to explain the cane. Tattoo Face seemed not to notice.

"Blade's on till two!" he shouted after me.

I raised a hand in thanks for the reminder, but I was still mulling the *talks to himself* part. The *over and over* sounded like chanting.

Add them up and I'd found my conjurer.

3

On the sixth floor, the demon stink was back. And gut-rottingly potent. I called more light to my cane and advanced on the door at hallway's end, weathered floorboards creaking underfoot.

The knob turned in my grasp, but one or more bolts were engaged. Crouching, I sniffed near the dark door space and immediately regretted the decision. "Holy *hell*," I whispered against my coat sleeve. The sickly-sweet scent burned all the way up to my brain, like ammonia.

Drawing the sword from my cane, I pointed it at the door and uttered, *"Vigore."*

A force shot down the length of the blade and snapped the bolts. The door blew inward. With another incantation, the light from my staff slid into a curved shield. I crouched, ready for anything, but except for the vibrating coming from one floor down, the space beyond the door was still and silent.

I tested the threshold with the tip of my sword. It broke the plane cleanly, which meant no warding spells.

Odd...

I entered, sword and glowing staff held forward. The unit was a restored tenement that, like many in the East Village, had been written off in the Crash's rumbling wake and left to die. Shadows climbed and fell over a newspaper-littered living room. I crept past sticks of curb-side furniture and a spill of canned goods before ducking beneath a line of hanging boxer briefs, still damp.

Hardly the evil-sorcerer sanctum I'd imagined.

I stuck my light into one of the doorless bedrooms, the silence tense against my eardrums. A thin roll-up mattress lay slipshod on a metal bed frame, dirty sheets puddled around its legs. A cracked window framed the bombed-out ruin of a neighboring building. When a pipe coughed, I wheeled, my gaze falling to a crowded plank-and-cinderblock bookcase.

In the light of my staff, I scanned book spines that might as well have read "Amateur Conjurer." Abrahamic texts, including a Bible, gave way to dime-store spell books and darker tomes, but without organization. Spaghetti shots in the dark. Someone looking for power or answers.

So where had the demon come from? More crucially, where had it gone?

In the neighboring bedroom, I flinched as my gaze met my own hazel eyes in a mirror on the near wall. *Gonna give myself a fricking heart attack*. Opposite the mirror, an oblong table held a scatter of spell-cooking implements. A Bunsen burner stood on one end, its line snaking to a tipped-over propane tank. Beside the tank, a pair of legs protruded.

I rounded the table and knelt beside the fallen conjurer. Parting a spill of dark, greasy hair, I took in a middle-aged male face with Coke-bottle glasses that had fallen askew, magnifying his whiskered right cheek. I recognized some of the conjurers in the city—or thought I did—and I'd never seen this guy. I straightened his glasses and patted his cheek firmly.

"*Hey,*" I whispered.

The man choked on a snort, then fell back into his mind-shattered slumber. He was alive, anyway.

I raised my light to the protective circle the man had chalked on the floorboards and no doubt stood inside while casting his summoning spell. A common mistake. Chalk made fragile circles. And a circle only protected spell casters capable of instilling them with power. That excluded most mortals, who weren't designed to channel, much less direct, the ley energies of this world.

They can damn sure act as gateways to other worlds, though.

My gaze shifted to a second circle near the table's far end, this one with a crude pentagram drawn inside. From a toppled pile of ash and animal entrails, a glistening residue slid into an adjacent bathroom.

Crap.

I felt quickly beneath the man's army surplus jacket and exhaled as my hand came back dry. The only reason he wasn't dead or mortally wounded was the recentness of the spell. Demonic creatures summoned from deeper down underwent a period of gestation, usually in a dark, damp space, to fortify their strength. They emerged half blind, drawn by the scent of the conjurer's vital organs, from which they derived even more potency.

That I'd arrived before that had happened was to my advantage. I hoped.

Rising, I crept toward the bathroom.

4

The trail turned dark red over the bathroom's dingy tiles, gobbets of black matter glistening in its wake. By now I was more or less desensitized to the smell, thank God. Through the half-open door, my light shone over a dripping faucet. The end of a free-standing tub glowed beyond.

With a foot, I edged the door wider.

The trail climbed the side of the tub, spread into a foul puddle, then climbed again. This time into a torn-out section of tiling between the shower head and the hot and cold spigots down below.

I adjusted my slick grip on the sword handle. The creature was inside the wall.

My sword hummed as I channeled currents of ley energy. With a *"Vigore!"* I thrust the sword toward the hole.

Tile and plaster exploded over my light shield in a dusty wave. A keening cry went up. In the exposed wall, wedged behind oozing pipes, I saw it. The creature had enfolded its body with a pair of membranous black wings. From a skull-sharp head of bristling hair, a pair of albino-white eyes stared blindly. Before I could push the attack, the creature screamed again.

The jagged sound became a weapon. Waves as sharp as the creature's barbed teeth pierced my thoughts and fractured my casting prism. I was dealing with a shrieker. A lower demonic being but ridiculously deadly—even to wizards.

My light shield wavered in front of me, then burst in a shower of sparks. The energetic release thrust me backwards as the room fell dark, my right heel catching the threshold. A squelch sounded, followed by the shallow splash of the thing dropping into the tub.

I flailed for balance but went down. My right elbow slammed into the floor, sending a numbing bolt up and down my arm. When metal clanged off behind me, I realized I'd lost my sword.

Beyond my outstretched legs, claws scrabbled over porcelain.

I kick-scooted away, sweeping an arm back for my weapon.

Wings slapped the air, the wet sound swallowed by the shrieker's next cry. Abandoning my search, I thrust my staff into the darkness above my face. The end struck something soft. A claw hooked behind my right orbital bone before tearing away, missing my eyeball by a breath.

I felt the shrieker flap past me, still clumsy in its just-summoned state. No doubt going for the conjurer. But if I was going to stop it, I had to do something about the damned screaming.

Blood dribbled down the side of my face as I sat up. Praying the shrieker wasn't rounding back on me, I jammed a finger into each ear. With the screaming muted, I repeated a centering mantra. Within seconds, the mental prism through which I converted ley energy into force and light reconstituted. A white orb swelled from the end of my staff, illuminating the apartment once more. I quickly touched the staff to each ear, uttering Words of Power. Shields of light energy covered them like muffs, blocking out the shrieker's cries.

I scooped up my sword and raised both sword and staff, expecting to find the shrieker hunched over the splayed-out conjurer. But the conjurer was alone, the shrieker nowhere in sight. The animal entrails were missing from the summoning circle, though, meaning it had fed.

Not good.

I raised my light toward the windows to ensure they were still intact. Remembering the blown-open front door, I hurried to the main room, terrified the creature had gotten out and into the city's six-million-person buffet. I ducked beneath the clothesline and felt the newspapers at my feet gusting up. I spun to find the abomination flapping at my face.

"*Vigore!*" I cried.

The wave-like force from my sword blasted the shrieker into a corner of the ceiling. It dropped onto a radiator, then tumbled wetly to the floor. I repeated the Word, but the shrieker scrabbled behind a wooden chair and darted into the bedroom. The chair blew apart in its stead.

I pursued and, guessing the creature's next move, aimed my staff at the near window. "*Protezione!*"

The light shield that spread over the glass held long enough for the shrieker to bounce from it. The shrieker launched itself at the window beside it, but I cast first. More sparks fell away as it beat its wings up and down the protected window like a flailing moth.

"You're not going anywhere, you little imp."

Only it wasn't so little anymore. The bed jumped when the shrieker dropped onto the headboard, taloned feet gripping the metal bar. The white caul over its eyes was thinning, too, goat-like pupils peering out. As I crept nearer, the creature's appearance stirred in me equal parts fascination and revulsion. Its wings spread to reveal a wrinkled body mapped in throbbing black vessels.

Okay, now it was just revulsion.

The shrieker put everything into its next scream. The light energy over my right ear broke apart. A sensation like shattered glass filled my head. Hunching my shoulder to my naked ear, I threw my weight into a sword thrust and grunted as hot fluid sprayed over me.

The shrieker fell silent, staring at me as though trying to comprehend what I had done. Its eyes fell to the sword, which had skewered its chest and driven a solid inch into the wall behind it. But it wasn't enough to physically wound such creatures. They had to be dispersed.

"Disfare," I shouted, concentrating force along the blade.

The shrieker's wings trembled, then began to flail. Unfortunately, the more power it took to summon a creature into our world, the more power it required to send it back. And the homeless appearance of the conjurer aside, some damned powerful magic had called this thing up.

"Disfare!" I repeated, louder.

The shrieker thrashed more fiercely, the tarry fluid that bubbled from its mouth drowning its hideous cry. But its form remained intact. And I was pushing my limits, a lead-like fatigue beginning to weigh on my limbs. The shrieker's wings folded down, and a pair of bat-like hands seized the blade.

"What the...?"

The creature gave a pull and skewered itself toward me.

"Hey, stop that!" I yelled pointlessly.

I pressed my glowing staff against its chin, but with another tug, the shrieker was an inch closer. It snapped at my staff with gunky teeth, then swiped with a clawed hand, narrowly missing my reared-back face.

I considered ditching my sword, but then what? I wasn't dealing with flesh and blood here. The second the shrieker came off the hilt, it would reconfigure itself, becoming larger and more powerful. And if it overwhelmed me, the conjurer would be next, followed by the head-bangers one floor down. An image of the party as a bloody scene of carnage jagged through my mind's eye.

"DISFARE!" I boomed.

A tidal wave of energy burst from my mental prism, shook down the length of my arm, through my sword, and then out the creature. I squeezed my eyes closed as the creature's gargling shriek cut off and an explosion of foul-smelling phlegm nearly knocked me down.

There was a reason I'd waterproofed my coat, and it wasn't for the shiny look.

I opened my eyes to a steamy, tar-spattered room and exhaled. The shrieker was gone, cast back to its hellish pit.

But at a price.

The edges of my thoughts swam in creamy waves, a sensation that heralded the impending arrival of Thelonious. That incubus spirit I called up a decade ago? He was still around, clinging to my spirit like a parasite. Despite that he was thousands of years old, I pictured him as a cool cat in black shades and a glittering 'fro—probably because he shared a name with a famous musician. And my Thelonious had a jazzy way about him. As long as I didn't push my limits, I could keep him at bay. Cross that line, and I became a vessel for Thelonious's, ahem, festivities.

And yeah, I'd just crossed that line.

More creamy waves washed in. I would have to work quickly.

The demonic gunk was evaporating as I drew my sword from the wall. I cleaned the blade against the thigh of my coat, resheathed it, and then returned to the fallen conjurer. Still out. I shone my light over his table, pocketing samples of spell ingredients for later study.

"But where oh where is the recipe?" I muttered.

I stopped at the flaky ashes of what appeared to have been a piece of college-ruled paper. The spell must have contained an incineration component, meant to destroy evidence of its origin.

"Naturally."

Sliding my cane into the belt of my coat, I stooped for the conjurer. "Up you go," I grunted. His head lolled as I carried him into the bedroom. I set him on the mattress, arranged his arms and legs into a semblance of order, then shook out the sheet and spread it over him.

His mortal mind was blown, but not beyond repair.

I touched my cane to the center of his brow and uttered ancient Words of healing. He murmured as a cottony light grew from the remaining power in the staff. The healing would take time, which was just as well. In a few more minutes, I wouldn't be in much shape to question him.

"I'll be back in a couple of days," I told the snoring man.

The creamy waves crested, spilling into my final wells of free will. There was no good place to go now except away from people. I was turning to leave when my—or I should say, Thelonious's—gaze fell to the space beneath the bed. A half-full bottle of tannic liquid leaned against one of the legs.

I felt my lips stretch into a grin. *Bourbon,* Thelonious purred in his bass voice.

My final memory of that night, the fire of alcohol in my throat, was tottering down a hallway toward a shaking generator and the siren screams of a pink-haired punker named Blade.

Ooh, yeah...

AVAILABLE NOW!

As a scholar and spell-caster, Everson Croft knows his magic. But when a mysterious evil threatens New York City, will it be enough?

AUTHOR NOTES

"And that, kids, is how I met Tabitha..."

When I published *Demon Moon* and then its prequel, *Book of Souls*, I received more than a few emails asking if I was ever going to explain how Everson and Tabitha ended up together.

At the time, I thought I might slip in an anecdote here and there in subsequent books, but it never happened.

So when I decided to send out another prequel to my subscribers, the story was obvious. But there was also this ten year gap between the events of *Book of Souls* and *Demon Moon* that I wanted to shine a little light into as well. Why is Everson relationship shy? Why does he seem so isolated when we meet him in the main series? And so on. Hopefully some of those questions have been answered.

The adventures of Everson (and Tabitha) pick up in *Demon Moon, Prof Croft Book 1*.

I sincerely hope you'll continue the journey.

Best wishes,
Brad Magnarella

CROFTVERSE CATALOGUE

PROF CROFT PREQUELS

Book of Souls

Siren Call

MAIN SERIES

Demon Moon

Blood Deal

Purge City

Death Mage

Black Luck

Power Game

Druid Bond

Night Rune

Shadow Duel

Shadow Deep

Godly Wars

Angel Doom

SPIN-OFFS

Croft & Tabby

Croft & Wesson

BLUE WOLF

Blue Curse

Blue Shadow

Blue Howl

Blue Venom

Blue Blood

Blue Storm

SPIN-OFF

Legion Files

For the entire chronology go to bradmagnarella.com

ABOUT THE AUTHOR

Brad Magnarella writes good-guy urban fantasy for the same reason most read it...

To explore worlds where magic crackles from fingertips, vampires and shifters walk city streets, cats talk (some excessively), and good prevails against all odds. It's shamelessly fun.

His two main series, Prof Croft and Blue Wolf, make up the growing Croftverse, with over a quarter-million books sold to date and an Independent Audiobook Award nomination.

Hopelessly nomadic, Brad can be found in a rented room overseas or hiking America's backcountry.

Or just go to www.bradmagnarella.com

Made in the USA
Coppell, TX
28 March 2025